The McCray Parables: The Fountain of Truth

THE MCCRAY PARABLES

THE FOUNTAIN OF TRUTH

A NOVEL

JEREMY BURSEY

This novel is the massively overhauled second edition of the original *The Fountain of Truth* e-book (2015).

For more information about this and other books, including updates, revisions, permissions, promotions, and extra bonuses, please visit jeremybursey.com.

ISBNs: (e-book) 978-1-966546-00-9 | (paperback) 978-1-966546-01-6 | (hardcover) 978-1-966546-02-3

Published by Zippywings Books
Lake Worth, Florida

For all those who dream crazy dreams.

And my family. Maybe they'll read this someday.

Introduction

About "The Fountain of Truth"
(originally written for the 2015 standalone collection, with a few additional style edits)

Every year on Facebook, I like to republish a fable I had written on Christmas Eve 2005 about families eating together at a popular restaurant for the holidays while revealing shocking truths about themselves to the surprise of their companions and children. I'd written it during a season when I, myself, was waiting tables and serving drinks to families who wanted to celebrate the holidays in public, and I wondered how much truth they were hiding from each other. "The Fountain of Truth" is my interpretation of what that scene might look like if no one were to keep anything hidden from each other.

Now that we're coming on the tenth anniversary of that story's creation, I thought it would be fun to take it beyond Facebook's range and make it more accessible for not just those who live on my Facebook friends list, but for everyone interested in the idea. So, I've decided to port it to the e-book format. If you're reading this, and if you're reading this on Christmas Eve, I want to say thanks for spending your evening with the fountain of truth (the fountain) and *The Fountain of Truth* (the story collection) and remember to always stay truthful because liars suck.

Oh, and the other stories, "Christmas Log" and "St. Nick's Gym," are brand new. I wrote them to give this e-book, and the idea of the Christmas fable, some weight. But I'm also considering making this into a yearly series, depending on how much the readers want it. Let me know if you want more.

With that, enjoy all the truth ahead.

About The McCray Parables
(2021)

Note: The following passage contains mild spoilers, both for this book and its immediate sequel. Read with caution if you want to be completely surprised, or read after you finish this book if you want to be surprised about *The Fountain of Truth* only.

The year after I published the 2015 edition of *The Fountain of Truth* (so, 2016 if we're doing math), I started writing its follow-up, *Snow in Miami*. My plan was to do more of the same: write three holiday-themed fables, stuff them into an e-book collection, then release them to the public. If all went well, I'd finish the collection in a couple of weeks. Then I could return to whatever novel-in-progress I was working on until the following year when I'd start on the third collection of fables and do it all over again.

But, as I examined my ideas for the first story in the new collection, it became clear to me I would need an outside story to frame it, sort of like how *The Princess Bride* has a grandfather reading a book to his grandson to contextualize the adventure, romance, and conflicts ahead. Without the framing device, the story's ending would make little sense. So, while this seemed like an arbitrary addition on the surface, it created a new problem for me. If I wrote an outside narrator to tell just one story, then the other stories would seem out of place. And I didn't want anything out of place, so I considered how I could develop a greater story that would encompass all three stories into its narrative and present a holiday fable that embodies the entire collection, not just the ridiculous lesson I'd crafted for the first story.

To address this continuity problem, I came up with the viewpoint character Douglas McCray. We meet him in his driveway as he comes home to a family he doesn't fully understand, to deal with a holiday he doesn't fully appreciate. Right off the bat, we're not sure what to make of him, but then he's given the task to tell a Christmas story to his four-year-old stepson. Suddenly, he's like Grandpa from *The Princess Bride*. Sort of. More like a reluctant grandpa. But it's enough for us to understand his character and the stories he tells. By the time we reach the end of the story (and his three fables), we're happy for him. Mostly. He's learned something about himself as he tries to teach his family what he knows about Christmas. I feel like I've done my job.

But then I remembered *The Fountain of Truth*.

Snow in Miami was supposed to be the follow-up to that, not a standalone. That meant it should contain all the same hallmarks as *The Fountain of Truth*. But then, what's the point of writing a follow-up to *The Fountain of Truth* if it says nothing about Douglas McCray or his Christmas fable-telling habit? Better yet, what's the point of saying *Snow in Miami* follows *The Fountain of Truth* if there's no mention of our lead hero in that first book?

In my own form of character growth, I realized I couldn't have a complete series if the first book didn't include the series characters. So, this ~~2021~~ 2024 edition of *The Fountain of Truth* is a retelling of the 2015 classic stories, but through the introduction and lens of our new titular hero, Douglas McCray. In this story, we meet Douglas and his crazy cast of characters for the first time (no longer in his driveway, but now as he prepares for an office Christmas party on the morning of Christmas Eve). Because these stories were never meant to have a framing device until now, I kept this particular McCray story short and simple to prevent creating convoluted situations. But hopefully, you'll find it a fun introduction to the character as he goes from one holiday adventure to the next in future installments.

And if you do enjoy this first episode, please remember to visit my website at jeremybursey.com for news or links on *Snow in Miami* (late ~~2022~~ 2025, hopefully) and other future *The McCray Parables* episodes as they're announced and released.

About the Story Update
(2024)

It's now three years since I wrote the original introduction to *The McCray Parables*. Thanks to numerous delays, distractions, and the ongoing production of other non-holiday books, including my long-in-development adventure thriller *The Golden Paperweight* (coming in 2025, hopefully), I've been slow to finish this series opener. But I've finally reached an endpoint, and as long as nothing blows up, you should get your chance to read it in time for Christmas 2024.

But the story has gone well beyond my original intention.

For starters, the completed version of *The Fountain of Truth* was just half the length of its sequel, *Snow in Miami*, bringing it to the whopping length of a short novella. Because I wanted as much consistency among each title in the series as possible, I thought the new story was just too short. So, I wrote a second half called *Happy New Life* to balance the story better and to keep it closer to the length of *Snow in Miami*, not to mention to give readers the opportunity to find out what happens next.

My plan was to release *Happy New Life* as a standalone bonus story for my newsletter subscribers, but it became clear to me rather quickly that it needed to become part of the mainline story, as it bridges certain gaps between *The Fountain of Truth* and *Snow in Miami* that would leave events up to interpretation for any non-subscriber to my newsletter. So, it is now part of the main story, picking up where *The Fountain of Truth* leaves off, and begins in the second half of this book.

That said, I still wanted a bonus story for my newsletter subscribers, but obviously not one so long or detrimental to the main story. So, I came up with the idea for "The Elf and the Shoe," which is a standalone fable that Douglas McCray tells to get out of eviction for failing to pay his rent on time and takes place a couple of days after the events in *Happy New Life*. If you'd like to read this bonus story, please be sure to sign up for my newsletter, which you can access from my website, jeremybursey.com.

Note that signing up for my newsletter gets you access to all my exclusive stories, including *Read My Shorts: Volume 1* (available now, plus future editions of *Read My Shorts* as I release them, if I release more), and at least two exclusive novellas, a thriller and a coming-of-age story, once they become available, as well as "The Elf and the Shoe."

You can find out more about the newsletter on my website if you're interested.

Note: "The Elf and the Shoe" may not be available until Christmas Eve 2024.

Finally, a Note about the Use of Movie Titles and Brand Names

The McCray Parables tries to live mostly in a fictitious world, where popular names of real-life corporate entities get swapped with names familiar but ultimately different. In most cases, the story allows for a clean swap, and even though you will know exactly which entity the new name represents, it will still come across as fictitious.

However, sometimes, the story needs the real-life name to make sense. For example, in this story, I reference the Hallmark Channel. I first tried changing it to the "Trademark Channel," in part to keep the name familiar, but also to pay homage to a fictitious production company I made up when I was a teenager. But in reading it back, I realized no one would understand the context, so I switched it back to the original name. Likewise, because the three stories in *The Fountain of Truth* were originally independent of each other and independent of the greater narrative, I didn't have the same rules for swapping out brand names for them as I do for the larger story.

So, in those special cases, I left the original names alone.

And regarding movie titles, I don't think the story would make any sense if I used substitutes, so I've kept them as-is.

I don't anticipate this name flip-flop upsetting anyone, but I wanted to call it out before you assume I overlooked some continuity errors. While it's possible I've overlooked a few anyway (for example, writing the Angela character as a brunette in her opening scene and making her blonde everywhere else — fixed!), the mix of pseudo and real corporate names and movie titles is intentional. If this does upset you, blame the Hallmark Channel for being so iconic.

Okay, now you can start reading *The Fountain of Truth*. Enjoy.

The
Fountain
of
Truth

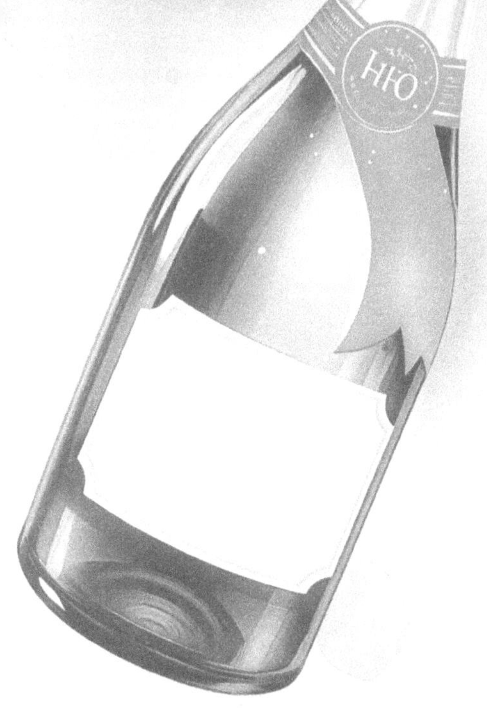

Chapter 1

Douglas McCray had heard of the concept of "The Christmas Miracle," but he didn't believe in that Hallmark Channel crap. As a student of reality and a champion of mediocrity, Douglas believed in just one holiday constant: "The Bah Humbug." It was the concept he had experienced for most of his life, and it was something he had no problem reliving year after year. It was like the wool blanket he slept under from December to March. Reliable and predictable. Exactly the way he understood his life, even if he didn't like it.

That wool blanket was covering him now as his squawking duck of an alarm clock harassed him out of his lovely, boring dreams. After thirty seconds of constant drubbing in his ears, Douglas reached out from under the blanket and swatted the clock off the nightstand. The noise changed elevation, but it did not stop. Now it was squawking from the floor.

"Bah Humbug," he said.

As the fog lifted from his head, he remembered that today was Monday, and that he could not sleep in if he cared about his job. Unfortunately, he cared about his job, so he waited for the alarm to stop on its own, spent another five minutes holding his pillow to his face as he contemplated whether he could sneak in just one more minute of sleep, then scolded himself for wasting the extra five minutes he could've spent standing under a hot shower.

It was time to get up.

As he slipped out of bed, he stepped on his alarm clock, nearly crushing it. He felt the plastic crack under the sole of his foot. It was an accident, he told himself, not at all intentional. Just another Monday.

He put the alarm clock on the table and checked his foot for injury. Because the plastic hadn't fully splintered, it didn't cut into his skin, so he was fine. No chance for bandaging it up or calling out sick. He cursed under his breath. It was time to leave the bed behind.

If the Christmas Miracle were a real thing, Douglas's wish would've come true by now. He'd have that vacation he wanted. He would not be going to work the Monday before Christmas, or in this year's case, the *day* before Christmas. And he would not be spending Christmas alone again for the tenth year in a row. Nevertheless, here he was, living the life he did not want. And his morning hangover started to hurt.

He shook his head. Stupid Hallmark Channel. He took his pants off and headed for the shower.

After unwrapping his cereal bar and stuffing it in his mouth, Douglas retrieved his favorite tie from the back of the sofa and twisted it tightly around his collar. As he secured the knot, something came scurrying through the crack in his mail slot and hit the carpet below.

It was much too early for a proper mail delivery, so the mysterious object couldn't have been the electric bill. Plus, it was alone, and bills rarely came through alone. And the people who always shoved fliers through, promoting their lame cover band performances on Saturday nights, wouldn't have been up before noon. So, whatever this was, it was different than usual, and it interested Douglas enough for him to check it out.

The envelope sat face-down by his front door. He flipped it over to find it unsealed and addressed to him by first name only. And there was no postmark. Just an envelope blank but for the hastily inked version of his name. The handwriting was familiar, but he couldn't place why. His curiosity grew.

He opened the door and checked down the hall for the delivery person. Whoever had brought it had already reached the stairs or entered another apartment. He wouldn't get his answers there.

Douglas closed the door and returned to the sofa with the envelope in hand. Because the flap was already loose, he slid the item inside halfway out. A cartoon image now facing him told more of the story.

Greeting him from inside the fold was a card with a picture of muscular Santa directing his elves to hammer nails into a bench press. There were no words printed over the image, but Douglas assumed he'd find some form of "Merry Christmas" on the inside.

He shuffled to the door and checked the hall again. Still empty. It had been so long since anyone had thought of him on Christmas Eve, who hadn't also asked for an end-of-the-year report, that he didn't know what to think or feel. He just stood there, staring in the direction of the elevator, until he remembered the clock was ticking. Who could have possibly given him a Christmas card on Christmas Eve, today?

Douglas dropped the card on the table and went to the kitchen for a cup of coffee. When he returned, he sat on the sofa and gave the card another look. On the front, Santa stood over the elf, pointing at the miserable creature with his left hand and raising his fist over his head with his right. The elf, who was hunched over the bench press as he watched Santa from over his shoulder, had sweat spewing from his face. In the muddy background, other elves were building other pieces of gym equipment, and from the topmost part of the card, a clumsy elf was tipping backward off a factory ledge while his arms flapped for balance recovery.

Douglas frowned. Seemed like an odd choice to demonstrate peace, love, and joy today. Very little about the card gave him the warm-and-fuzzies. If someone had wanted to change his mind about the holidays, the picture of Santa Claus exhibiting tyranny in the workshop didn't help. Perhaps the real message was on the inside. He flipped it open to get the rest of the story.

The card was blank save for six handwritten words:

You're a Grinch.
Signed Miss Nancy

Douglas smirked. Of course.

He closed the card and flung it across the room. Miss Nancy was his landlady. He'd paid his rent on time, and he never complained about his broken sink. So, she must not have liked what he'd put out in the trash last night. Even though this was the first time she'd gotten him a Christmas card, it wasn't the first time she'd sent him a scathing message through his mailbox about his lifestyle choices.

In retrospect, he should've known she was the delivery person all along. Probably not worth picking up.

A minute passed before he realized he was staring at the coffee table. He'd already wasted too much time on this. If he didn't leave now, he'd be late for work. At least there, people appreciated him more. A little more. At least a little more than Santa appreciated his elves.

Bah Humbug, he thought.

Most of Douglas's coworkers were not fans of the Bah Humbug school of thought. They were the unrealistic types who weren't exactly believers in Santa Claus or anything but were believers in the Christmas Miracle, whatever that was. Even at work on a Monday, they suffered from a condition called "The Christmas Spirit," which Douglas understood as the psychotic joy one feigned when hearing "Jingle Bells" or seeing a tree decked in lights. It didn't matter where they were, either. Even from behind a cluttered desk and a computer monitor adorned in blinking spreadsheets, they would sing at their neighbors, "Ho-Ho-Ho," and not even mean it as an insult.

Chief among those cheerful liars was his boss, Angela Prince. For 327 days out of the year, Angela was a whip-cracker and butt-kicker, seen rarely without folded arms over her chest or a scowl on her face. From January 6th to December 9th, she was the company's helicopter mom who believed she was the only one smart enough to do the job right, and anyone trying to prove otherwise would endure a terrible humiliation via a public lecture on the office floor. But from December 10th to December 24th, she was the company's happiest elf, decorating the office with lights and streamers, bringing in coffee and donuts each day, signing improvement request notes with a little heart and candy cane. From December 25th to January 5th, she was on vacation.

Seeing Angela standing at his desk with a plate of cookies in hand made Douglas's neck throb. He had just entered the office, ignored the receptionist when she said hello, and veered past the potted plant between the reception area and the cubicle farm when he rounded the corner and saw Angela standing there. Because his desk was closest to the bathrooms, which were closest to the potted plant, he had no time to avoid her. She was poised with her knotted blonde hair, her purple lipstick, and her holidays-only smile pointing right at him, signaling it was time for him to work but also time to get fat.

"They're caramel peppermint," she told him as she handed him the plate. "Baked with love."

Douglas set his briefcase on the desk.

"What's that supposed to mean?"

"Secret ingredient. You'll find out after the Secret Santa party." She eyed his briefcase, then looked at him. Her smile had gone sterile. "You did remember to bring a gift today, didn't you?"

Douglas squeezed the edges of his lips tight, shut his eyes, and nodded.

"Of course, I remembered." He'd completely forgotten. Too much Scotch and cola over the weekend. "It's in the car. I'll bring it in later. No sense in ruining the surprise early, right?"

"Glad to hear it." She checked the clock on the wall. "And thank you for getting here during the first fifteen minutes of your shift."

"Merry Christmas," Douglas said.

Angela wandered off toward some other unfortunate soul—looked like Terrance Walker's desk. Douglas sat down and forbade himself to look in her direction any longer.

Instead, he opened his briefcase to check his inventory. Because he borrowed his work supplies for his home office, he wasn't sure which tools he'd remembered to repack. As he rummaged through his stash, mentally separating his office supplies from his personal ones, he checked off the stapler, calculator, paperweight, and mechanical pen, and set each one on his desk. He'd forgotten his paper clips, reading glasses, earbuds, and scissors.

Not wanting to spend the day unprepared, he ducked over to Winston Field's desk in the next cubicle for the extra supplies. Winston had enough items scattered about that he wouldn't notice his paper clips or scissors missing. Then again, Winston was a keen observer of unnoticeable things, which came in handy whenever he balanced his sales figures. So, he might've noticed. Either way, whatever clips he didn't use, Douglas vowed to put back at the end of the day *in case* Winston noticed. Assuming he'd remember, of course.

Once he settled in, Douglas turned on his desktop monitor and checked his email. Of the ten messages he had waiting, three were from Angela wishing him and the team a Merry Christmas. They all ended with the same reminder:

Don't forget to bring your Secret Santa on Monday.

The most recent reminder was sent twenty minutes ago. Douglas deleted it. He'd buy something during his lunch break.

Just after eleven o'clock, Douglas McCray rolled his chair out of his cubicle, swiveled around, and sprang forward into the men's room. It was a literal three-step process requiring hardly any physical movement. Once inside, it was another three-step process to the urinal, but with longer strides required. The total distance from his desk to the urinal was maybe twenty feet. Perfect location for the highest efficiency and closest emergencies.

It was also the perfect location for disappearing or getting some exercise. He didn't have to use the bathroom per se, but he did need to stretch his legs, and taking a walk to the urinal gave him that excuse. It was also a great way to avoid Angela in the event she wanted to talk to him. He always sensed her near, even when she was in her office.

The problem with being so close to his desk, however, was that the time he spent in the bathroom was the only time he could spend away from his desk. Once he opened the door, the adventure was already over. That moment of peace and sanity would again segue into madness or depression.

As he finished his business and cleaned his hands, he looked in the mirror and frowned. Another morning consumed by meaningless tasks, to pay for an apartment he hated living in, to spend his nights inside with no one to share his space or time with, all made worse by another holiday that sucked his heart dry. He shook his head as he studied his face. At least his tie was on straight.

And then came a Christmas Miracle.

Douglas stepped out of the restroom and was prepared to plop back in his chair when he heard an unfamiliar but melodious voice coming in from the reception area. It was possible he also heard jazz playing in the background, but it was equally possible he heard it only in his head.

New voices were a distraction, especially when they came from a higher octave than his own, and Douglas told himself on many occasions to ignore all the voices he couldn't confirm. But he was bad at taking his own advice, and he was worse at prioritizing his job over more interesting things like melodious voices coming from reception, and given his version of the "Christmas Spirit," he thought anything that bought him extra time away from work was a gift.

So, he skipped the chair and tiptoed to the potted plant to have a look.

When he peeked around the corner, his jaw dropped. Leaning against the reception desk was the loveliest brunette in a blue skirt he'd seen in years, peddling some printed mockup materials she had propped up on the counter with her forearm. Unfocused thoughts suddenly blasted through his mind. If he'd been thinking even a little of his spreadsheets before, he wasn't giving them any brain power now.

The woman was too busy persuading the receptionist for an audience to take notice of Douglas, but she'd certainly gotten his notice. Her presence was too nonstandard for a place like this, and too exciting for him to pass up the opportunity to get her attention. It was like opening the door to an industrial warehouse and discovering a lush paradise of gardens and sunshine inside. It would've been impossible to look in without also being drawn to enter. Douglas knew nothing of this beautiful stranger, but he wanted to know everything. And observing her in secret was no way to learn anything of value. So, he popped out from behind the plant, extended his hand, realized he hadn't dried it very well, wiped it on his shirt, then extended it again.

"Douglas," he said. As far as he knew, his breath was serviceable. But he snatched a peppermint off the receptionist's desk just in case.

The woman glanced at him, clearly surprised by his apparitional appearance. She'd almost dropped her books on the receptionist's lap when she struggled to free her own hand for the handshake.

"Miranda," she said. "Are you the manager here?"

He raised his eyebrows at her.

"Better," he said. What was he even saying to her right now? And did it matter?

She mirrored his expression.

"Board member?"

"Better." He winked.

She smiled.

"Don't listen to this fool," a voice said from behind the floor plant.

Everyone turned. Terrance Walker shuffled into the reception area, movements so exaggerated that his long hair swished along the side of his face. He brushed Douglas aside and extended his hand for the handshake. When Miranda took it, he tipped her hand to his lips and kissed the back of it. She withdrew and wiped it on her blouse.

"Terrance Walker, manager in charge," Terrance said. "How can I help you?"

"Well, I was just telling your receptionist—"

Terrance put his finger on her lips, shook his head, and shushed her.

"Don't care about the receptionist." He glanced at Sally the receptionist and mouthed the words *not true* at her. "The question is, how can I help *you*?"

Miranda backed away from his finger and raised the books so he could see.

"I'm a representative for the Corporate Instructional Group at Regency, or CIGAR for short. Your company showed up on our register."

"Ah, yes," Terrance said. "I love a good register. Shall we discuss this further over dinner?"

Miranda gave him a blank stare.

"I'm not sure that's necessary," she said. "A conference room would be fine. Now perhaps?"

Terrance nodded.

"True. True. But you must be hungry. How about lunch?"

"I'm fine, really," she said. "I'm just here to—"

Douglas stepped in between Miranda and Terrance. He glared at Terrance before giving his attention to Miranda.

"Perhaps I can supervise this meeting. Make sure you get the sale you're quite obviously here to make." He looked at Terrance again for clarification. *Back off my woman* was Douglas's secret message to him. Terrance gave him a tight smile. It appeared he was bouncing Douglas's statement right back at him.

"Yes, that would be nice," Miranda said.

Douglas returned his gaze at her and smiled.

"Excellent. Do you prefer Italian or Chinese?"

Miranda shrugged.

"The conference room is perfectly fine."

Douglas closed his eyes and nodded once. "Italian it is."

<h1 style="text-align:center">Chapter 2</h1>

T̲HE RESTAURANT WAS ALREADY busy when Douglas, Miranda, and Terrance took their table twenty minutes before noon. Well, busy for its size. It was a modest Italian place with arches over doorways, plants perched in small alcoves along the hallways into each dining room, and a small café and bar area just inside the foyer. Its hosts wore dark slacks and white long-sleeved dress shirts. The servers were dressed similarly but had green aprons around their waists and carried wine bottles with them to every table, offering samples even at lunch, all to celebrate "the taste of Italy." They also served a basket of garlic and butter breadsticks on delivery with the drinks.

After Douglas, Miranda, and Terrance took their seats—Miranda had sat down first, and the other two fought over who would sit beside her until she told them both to sit across from her—the server showed up with a bottle and three wine glasses. He had the name "Valiant" displayed on ticker tape over his shirt pocket.

"Welcome to Olive Farm," Valiant said. "Would you like to sample our signature red wine today?" It was still before noon.

"We're on the job," Miranda said.

"And I still have a bit of a hangover from last night," Douglas said.

"I'll take one," Terrance said.

Once the breadsticks and waters arrived, Miranda diminished Douglas's small talk and got down to business.

"Because you haven't yet created a membership with us, I think you would benefit from learning about our services."

"Who are you with again?" Douglas asked.

"CIGAR."

"Ah, right. What's the deal with CIGAR?"

"Wait," Terrance said. "We should toast to our fortunate meeting." He raised his wine glass, which he'd topped off after liking the sample. "To us."

Douglas shrugged. He didn't see the point to this. Neither he nor Terrance had the power to buy anything from this woman since the real acquisitions manager, Angela, was back at the office, and neither one wanted the other to be here. Toasting their "good fortune" seemed counter to the truth. Nevertheless, he didn't like being a poor sport. He held up his water glass a few inches and waited for Miranda to lift hers.

Before Miranda could reach for her own glass—if she'd even bothered to move—Terrance lightning-struck Douglas in the crotch from under the table. It was so fast that Douglas couldn't tell if he'd balled up his fist or knuckled him from a flat hand, but it was sharp enough to send such a jolt of pain through his system that it caused him to drop his water on his lap. Terrance leapt out of his seat to avoid getting drenched.

"Whoa, mama." Terrance swiveled to Miranda's side of the table to keep himself dry. "You should see if they got a hand dryer in the bathroom to take care of that wet mess on your pants."

Douglas gave Terrance the evil eye. Miranda was too busy tossing her napkins at him to notice the exchange.

"Soak it with these," she said.

"Since it'll take you a while to dry off," Terrance said, "what do you want us to order for you?"

Douglas shook his head and smiled. He took his wet napkins and plopped them right on Terrance's breadstick.

"I'm fine. I'll dry faster sitting right here." He glanced at Miranda. "So, tell us more about CIGAR."

Terrance grumbled under his breath as the social distraction rolled away to make room for business. As soon as Miranda broke into her spiel, Terrance's eyes wandered off and gazed at other tables, especially the one two tables away. A couple of attractive twenty-somethings were laughing about something, and Terrance was spending most of Miranda's presentation staring at them.

The gist of her job was to sell them customized instruction manuals they could gift or resell to their clients. The idea was to stack their reception table with books about their business and services, giving the public a better understanding of what they offered. Depending on the service, they could also make premium information available to potential partners for a set price. To make that possible, her company would convert a 5,000-words-or-less manuscript into printable texts visitors could take and read or discard while having the answers to any of their questions at their fingertips. This would include providing them with booklets and brochures in case the larger form books were too dense.

When Douglas asked how that was better than just creating a website, she told him her company could do that, too.

"But studies show that people are more likely to read a printed book than they are an entire website," she said. "You can provide the information much faster and a lot cheaper online. But that's only if they're looking for it, or if you advertise for it, which can ultimately cost you far more. With books, booklets, and brochures, anyone who visits your business can get the same information, but because they made the effort to show up, they're more likely to read your words. Not only that, but you don't have to commit to additional marketing to reach them since they're already curious enough about you to walk in the door."

"And that works?"

"That's how I found your company. I thought, 'Hey, what do these people do?' I still don't know the answer, but after you invest in our service, I'll find out what you do, and so will your potential customers."

"We specialize in fertilizer sales," Douglas said. "Our clients are mostly farmers who live a hundred miles away. We also service laboratories and influencers on the dark web."

Her face went sour at that last bit.

"So now you know," Douglas said.

"Is that true?" she asked.

"Is it true that we sell fertilizer? Yes."

"To people on the dark web?"

"We mostly service farmers, from my understanding. Management doesn't answer all our questions."

She shook her head.

"Wait, aren't *you* management?"

Douglas's stomach dropped as he realized what he'd just said. When he glanced at Terrance for help, he was unsurprised to find him still watching the attractive twenty-somethings, completely and psychologically removed from his own party.

"Terrance?" Douglas said. "Why aren't you paying attention to the conversation?"

Terrance ignored him.

Miranda folded her arms over her chest. "Are you management or not?"

Douglas rolled his eyes. He checked the status of his glass. The server still hadn't come back to take their orders or issue him a replacement drink. But there was enough of a puddle remaining that he could quench the heat building in his mouth. He sipped what was left.

"The answer to that question is complicated."

"Okay, here's another question. Do you have *any* authority to negotiate or sign a publishing contract with CIGAR?"

Douglas stirred around his now-empty glass. Where was that server, anyway?

"Terrance?"

His coworker ignored him. In fact, he was edging his way out of the booth.

"Terrance!"

Terrance was now fully out and standing. He turned to apologize.

"Sorry, don't know what you're talking about. Two honeys at ten o'clock. Gotta check 'em out."

He slipped over to the table with the two attractive twenty-somethings and sat beside the prettier one. Both girls choked their conversation out of existence and displayed looks of confusion on their faces.

"What authority do you actually have?" Miranda asked.

Douglas closed his eyes.

"It's complicated."

"Please look at me when you're lying."

Douglas looked at her.

"I'm not lying."

The server finally returned with a new glass of water. He set it before Douglas, taking the older, mostly empty one away.

"Are you folks ready to order?"

"That depends on how he answers my next question," Miranda said. She leaned toward Douglas. "How are you not lying?"

Douglas glanced at her, then at his water, then at the server.

It suddenly occurred to him there was no straight answer he could give that would satisfy her. So, he said the first thing that came to mind.

"Christmas Miracle."

"What?"

That was a dumb answer, he realized. He glanced at Terrance, who was now chatting up the two attractive twenty-somethings, even though neither looked happy to listen. The other tables were full of people displaying similar expressions of sadness or indifference. No one here looked particularly pleased with their company. It reminded Douglas of the one truth he did know.

"Okay," he said. "I owe you the real truth. The truth is—"

Douglas understood the best way to communicate his thoughts about a situation was to express it through an associative lens, like a moral, or a parable.

"Everyone's a phony," he said.

Miranda leaned back against her seat. The server stared at him as if in shock.

"Let me explain," Douglas continued.

The Fountain of Truth

THE KINGDOM AFFAIR RESTAURANT in the upper section of town was world-renowned for its ritzy atmosphere, its genteel clientele, and its popularity among holidays. Established from the skeleton of an old ballroom at the base of a glamorous hotel, the restaurant developed a style of high-class living that rivaled the aristocracy, the wealth, and the social gatherings of the posh sort. It was the perfect locale to usher in the Rolls Royce of façades when the name of saving face was in order.

For this wealthy establishment, Christmas Eve was regarded as the busiest night of the year. On this eve of holidays, families and cohorts of the upper-class persuasion dined to their hearts' content, laughing and chatting over things that bore little significance to their lives. Dominating conversational topics ranged from pools, to spas, to Mercedes brand automobiles—all delivered through smiles that masked what people truly thought of the world. It was colorful bliss of the richest kind.

But on this particular Christmas Eve, something remarkable happened. All across the restaurant, from one wall to the other, from the big room to the private one, the façade somehow fell. Families and friends abandoned their discussions of plastic surgery and million-dollar homes to speak of life in its truest colors. Those who were sobered were stunned. *How dare they speak their mind?* they thought, as sincerity erupted from out of nowhere and threatened to unsettle their special little utopian thoughts.

The first sign of this Christmas miracle began with a table of eight—four men, four women—all wearing thousand-dollar outfits and million-dollar smiles. They had just taken their seats, the drinks had already arrived, and the hors d'oeuvres were on the way when the first break in conversation occurred.

"And the Jaguar drives like a dream," laughed the first man, a frail gray-haired chap of about seventy. "I haven't been so happy since I got my latest Botox injection."

He took a sip of his soft drink, which he had ordered to keep from mixing his medication with alcohol.

"But then, what's a Botox injection," he continued, "but to mask my decrepit state and my inability to compete with the young men of today?"

The rest of the table gasped with astonishment. Where did this insult to the miracle of chemicals and plastic come from? The old man next to him *tsked* his tongue at him.

"What kind of question is that?" he asked. "Botox gave me new life."

He took a sip of his own soft drink.

"A new life," he continued, "to show me how discouraged I was with my old life . . . a life spent with a woman I never loved, who grew old on me ten years into marriage and was no longer the trophy I was proud of."

The woman next to him gasped with angry surprise.

"Trophy wife?" she said. "Is that what I've been to you for forty years? A trophy wife? I loved you with all my heart and this is how you repay me?"

She took a sip of her own soft drink to clear her rapidly drying throat.

"I mean, I lied to you night and day so you wouldn't divorce me and kick me out of your will. Do you realize how much I endured to pretend my love was real so I could have all your money when you die? I put up with your bad breath and your smelly feet for forty years, because I wanted to be rich, and now you have the nerve to call me a trophy wife? How dare you?"

And that wasn't the only place this miracle unfolded. On the other side of the restaurant, in a broader space, a family of three shared a table, awaiting the arrival of their prime steak dinners. The father, a young strapping man in his mid-thirties, the mother, a young, beautiful woman made of diamonds and pearls, and the ten-year-old boy made of oatmeal and cookie dough, all sat around with soft drinks in hand, discussing the wonderful day they were about to have.

"You're going to love all your toys," said the father to the son, with such glorious pride that his smile flashed halfway across the room. "I don't want to tell you everything I bought, but I promise it will be grander than last year's big one hundred."

The father took a sip of his soft drink.

"Because," he continued, "I don't want to show you just how inadequate of a father I am, so I have to do my part to buy your love, which I know I can't do, because I'm shaping you into a young spoiled brat, but I don't want to take the time away from my business to be with you, so I figure that buying all these toys will hide my guilt, and that your mother will think I'm a good father and in turn respect me, which I know deep down she doesn't, because I hear her muttering unsavory things at night in her sleep, but that's okay, because I know I can buy her love, too, as long as I keep the fine jewelry coming."

And again, the table gasped, but this time the young impressionable heart and the soft, yet jewelry-covered woman both sobbed at the revelation that things weren't what they seemed and that façades had taken control.

Eventually, the young mother, after taking several sips of her own soft drink, said, "Maybe we need help."

Restaurant staff members—always keen observers of the way high society operated within those walls—were astonished at all the truth unfolding before them. Table after table swept up in a rage, while others floated off in a stream of tears. Meals were sent back as steaks and pork chops went uneaten from lost appetites or had just gotten cold from being unattended to for so long. Drinks continued to arrive because throats kept running dry from all the shouting, but the truths didn't stop, and the hearts kept exploding. When the head chef finally asked if anything environmental had changed to cause such an outburst of reality, one server by the name of Valiant spoke up with bright eyes and a steady demeanor.

"I thought the greatest gift I could give these people," he said, "was the gift of truth. So, I injected the soft drink syrup with a vial of serum I bought from the mall, and now every guest has consumed it unknowingly. Even though I've ruined Christmas for most of them, I delivered them from their phony existence, and now they can live truthfully again."

As the head chef looked at him with astonishment, Valiant took another sip of his favorite soft drink, which he had forgotten he had tampered with just ten minutes earlier.

Chapter 3

WHEN DOUGLAS FINISHED HIS story, he nodded at the server, Valiant, and told him his work was done. Valiant's eyes shifted from side to side. The remaining liquid in Douglas's mostly finished glass trembled within Valiant's grip. He marched off past the plants stiff legged. Something in the man's retreat caused Douglas to cock an eyebrow. He swirled his new glass, checking it for discoloration or chemical reactions with the side of the glass.

"Hope my story wasn't actually true," he said.

"So, what you're telling me," Miranda said, "is that you're lying to me to make me happy?"

"Isn't that the only reason anyone lies?"

Miranda stretched her arms before her and studied her pink nails.

"What would make me happy is if you had the power to buy my books so I can keep my job and finish paying for nursing school. Whatever this thing is you're doing about bringing me here without any intention of buying my books or allowing me to preserve my job is not exactly helpful." She leaned forward and drilled into his sights. "You do understand this, right?"

"You're studying to be a nurse?"

"You understand this, right?" she said again.

Douglas shrugged. He understood she was upset about the obvious lie, but he didn't understand why she couldn't appreciate his reasons.

Then it occurred to him he'd never actually told her his reasons.

"I'm attracted to you," he said, hoping to undig the hole he'd created.

Her eyebrows shot up.

"Excuse me?"

"I have no intention of buying your books. But I would like to know more about you. So, you're trying to become a nurse?"

Miranda was now thin-lipped. Douglas didn't know Miranda well enough to read her thoughts or expressions with confidence, but he guessed she was less than thrilled with his response and that he should've kept his mouth shut about his reasons. The art of courtship required finesse and time management. He'd demonstrated neither in the last few minutes.

He studied his drink again. Its taste and clarity suggested he was drinking water, but the bluntness of his words suggested the Valiant Special might've been real.

Douglas pushed his glass away just in case.

"Let's start over," he said. "My name is Douglas, I'm a sales rep for a fertilizer distribution company, and you have my attention."

"It seems I also have your fertilizer," Miranda said.

Douglas couldn't help but laugh at that one. Her assessment was true, but she wasn't laughing with him. He'd still have to correct the situation.

Then he remembered a small detail she'd mentioned when she'd first shook his hand, and suddenly he found his footing in this exchange.

"How did you say you found us again?" he asked.

"I was curious about your company, so I walked in." She'd said it with a straight face.

Douglas smiled. *Everyone's a phony.*

"Didn't you say you found us on a business register earlier?"

Miranda said nothing. She studied him for another few seconds, then glanced away. Douglas let her stare into the void a little longer.

"Right," he said when the silence had made its point. "So, once again, let's start over. I'm Douglas, and I'm a sales rep who is interested in helping you out somehow."

When lunch ended, Douglas admitted he didn't have any buying power within the company, but he would attempt to pair Miranda with the person who did if she agreed to overlook his deception. He told her that, in the event her sale failed, she could blame Terrance for the fallout since lunch was technically his idea. He also assured her he would've been perfectly happy working with her back at the reception desk had Terrance stayed out of it. Miranda agreed to the terms.

Even though the three of them had ridden to the restaurant together, Douglas thought it was in their best interest to leave Terrance behind—he was still trying to plead his own case with the two attractive twenty-somethings who were both sneering at his every word—so he and Miranda drove back to the office alone together. Miranda was certainly resistant in sharing any personal detail with him, and given the short drive, she wouldn't have gotten much time to share anything of value, anyway. But Douglas still did everything possible to probe even the basics out of her, like how old she was, what her favorite Christmas movie was, assuming she liked Christmas movies, and what she thought about his car to name a few things. Each answer seemed to soften her disposition toward him a little, and the nagging awareness that his pants were still wet restrained him from asking anything risky, but her stiff shoulders suggested there was still ice to break from her skin.

"I'm not a big fan of Christmas," Douglas said, when she bounced his own questions back at him. "Never saw a movie I particularly liked, except for maybe that one about the dad who got stuck dangling from the roof when he missed a step putting lights along the eaves."

"*Christmas Vacation*," she said. "Chevy Chase. Love that movie."

Douglas sensed an opportunity here. He had been hunched over his steering wheel, dreading every block that brought him closer to the office, but hearing her voice shift in an upward pitch convinced him he should perk up and respond in kind.

"Yeah, me too!"

Silence befell them. Nothing about his excitement registered as genuine, and he could sense the falseness in his voice. Even if she didn't know much about him, it wouldn't take her long to figure out when he was lying. The actual truth was he thought the movie was fine but not great. It was just the only one he didn't hate.

"Still prefer *Die Hard*, though," Douglas said when things got too quiet. "I think it qualifies as a Christmas movie. Part of an unending debate."

Miranda nodded.

"I'm not a big fan of bloody action movies," she said, "but I do like that one. It captures the full spectrum of the human condition."

Douglas hadn't thought of it that way.

"What do you mean?"

"Well, you have this cop—a man about the law, and everyone wants order in their society—who gets off a plane—landing safely is the number one desire for anyone who flies, seeking the anchor of land, so to speak—"

Douglas nodded at her. He wondered if she would end up critiquing the entire move from start to finish, and if he should try to participate in the conversation by adding his own piece to it, just to keep from looking like an idiot later.

"Yeah," he said, "and he enters the airport where he fights a tide of human beings—resistance—and watches a blonde lady leap into the arms of a stranger—risk and reward—and finds a limousine—prosperity—and—"

"I don't think the blonde lady is leaping into the arms of a stranger," Miranda said. "I'm sure they know each other."

Douglas shrugged.

"We don't know that. We're made only to assume that. How do we know she wasn't seeking out the most attractive dude at the airport and that's the guy she deemed worthy?"

"I don't think it's actually relative to the plot, but—"

"No, no, let's investigate this. Who's the blonde lady, who's the dude, and do they actually know each other, or are they made only to appear as if they know each other when in reality that's the first time they've met?"

"I suppose it's possible the actors met for the first time that day. I mean, they're extras. It wouldn't be that unusual. But the characters I'm sure knew each other."

"But you can't be sure. We're not given that information."

Miranda shook her head. Now she was looking out the window and the city shopfronts racing by. Douglas was losing her.

"Let me clarify," he said. "Maybe they do know each other. I'm sure at some point they will know each other. But one thing's for sure." He waited for Miranda to look at him before finishing his thought. "They know each other now. And they're probably in love."

Miranda rolled her eyes and chuckled.

"Sure. The movie is over thirty years old. I doubt they're in love."

"But they gave love a chance."

"Maybe."

Douglas nodded. He had Miranda on the hook now. At least the idea of love and the future was in her head.

"When we get back," he said, "the person you need to sell your books to is Angela Prince. Make sure you say everything you know about Christmas. Angela's a sucker for the holiday. It's the only way you stand a chance with her. And if possible, try to introduce yourself to Gordon Riche. His dad owns the company, and he's got the power to sway Angela's decisions. Sometimes."

Miranda glanced back at him and smiled.

"Thanks," she said.

Douglas smiled back. *Now* he had her on the hook.

Chapter 4

As soon as Douglas had gotten back to the office, he introduced Miranda to Angela, who was fortunately patrolling the office floor for updates on everyone's projects, wished Miranda luck, and stepped aside to offer her the floor. Miranda shook Angela's limp hand, then produced the first book. Even though Angela demonstrated zero interest in entertaining her sales pitch, Miranda was too busy pointing at the mockup photos in her prototype to notice her fidgeting fingers and tapping left foot.

Douglas, however, spotted it immediately. Miranda was losing the sale before she could break the first layer of ice off Angela's heart, so he stepped in and, through a whisper to Angela's ear, offered to work until late into the evening if she'd take the pitch seriously.

Angela pulled him aside.

"These contracts are expensive," Angela warned him. "There's no room in the budget for them."

"Of course there is," Douglas said. "There's always room. Maybe it'll take creativity, but we can find a way."

"Yeah? Should I start with cutting your salary in half?"

Douglas groaned at the suggestion.

"There are other ways," he said. "For example, maybe we could turn the heater off when we leave the office. How much will that cut down on our electric?"

"Would you like to be the one to come in at five in the morning to turn it back on?"

This wasn't working.

"Look, we can find a solution that benefits everyone. We don't have to attack me personally to make it work. What do we have around here that we don't need?"

"Want me to give you their names or just their titles?"

Douglas glared at her.

"Angela. It's Christmas. Could you work with me on this one?"

Angela's plastic expression warmed up a little. A tiny smile crossed her face.

"Yes, you're right. It's Christmas. Tell me, why do you suddenly care about marketing materials?"

"I always care about marketing materials."

"You didn't show any interest when that last representative was here to pitch a packet of sales materials to us."

Douglas drew a blank.

"When was that?"

"Three weeks ago."

He had no such memory of the incident.

"Was I here?"

"Of course you were here. You walked right past the guy. Went straight to Gordon's office for some reason."

Douglas shrugged.

"No idea. But this one's important. Just listen to her, please? Maybe you'll decide her offer is a good one."

They both glanced at Miranda, who was pacing the floor by the plant, checking her watch, and biting her lip.

"Okay, here's the deal," Angela said. "Because it's Christmas, I will listen to the pitch. But I want no distractions, got it?"

"I'd be happy to advise if—"

Angela jabbed her finger at his chest.

"No distractions. I need to listen to every word and consider every variable. If I think for a moment this contract is bad for the company, I will not accept it. But if she can convince me, I'll run it by Gordon for consideration and approval."

Douglas relaxed.

"Thank you."

Angela took one step toward Miranda, then stopped. She eyed Douglas suspiciously.

"Seriously, why do you care so much about this sales package?"

"Because I see value in it."

Angela shook her head, clearly disbelieving him.

"I remember you caring about our vendors' products only twice before."

"They were good products."

"Sure they were. You hadn't spoken about either of them since."

Douglas said nothing.

Angela once again pointed at him. "Remember, no distractions. And you agree to stay late tonight to finish those spreadsheets."

"I said I would."

The offer worked. Angela returned to Miranda and suggested they continue the discussion in the conference room. The conference room was usually empty right after lunch, and today was no different. Once they were inside, Angela had made it clear to Douglas one last time not to bother them and that he was committed to fulfilling his promise. Angela had a habit of ensuring her message was unforgettable.

She made a quick phone call. Then she kicked him out.

The meeting would remain private. No interference. No additional persuasion. Within moments of the door closing and the company's chief security guard and Angela's personal bouncer, Harvey, taking position, several staff members learned by experience that whatever emergency they had, it could wait. One by one he turned them away, Lena, Larry, Tyson, Billy. Did they need a signature? Didn't matter. Did they need advice on how to handle an account discrepancy? Screw off. The conference room, normally a vacant and unimpressive space for dust to settle, was now the office's inner sanctum for urgent decision-making, and within its walls was a deal of utmost importance.

Douglas had done his part to help Miranda, but he nevertheless longed to be on the inside. From where he sat, he could neither see Miranda nor monitor her progress with Angela. He had just the view of an empty piece of the table. Even though the door was transparent, the surrounding windows had obstructions. Inside, parts of the room were adorned in venetian blinds, drawn to conceal all activities within. On the outside, a potted plant barrier flanked each glass panel. But even with the see-through door, there wasn't much of a view thanks to Harvey blocking it.

So, Douglas was left sitting at his desk, staring at his spreadsheets, having little more than his imagination to inform him about what transpired inside. Would Miranda make her sale? Would she exit the room so happy with the outcome that she'd run over and thank Douglas for his help, or squeeze his shoulder in appreciation of his intervention, or grab a tuft of his hair, thrust his head back, and plant a full-on open mouth kiss lasting for several minutes as a form of gratitude for the connection he'd given her? Or would she storm out, cursing the names of every representative, manager, and service personnel who worked there, along with whatever celebrity or political figure they worshipped?

Not knowing the answer to those questions left him tapping his fingers against the table and his brain viewing his spreadsheets as a blob of shapes, not the field of data entry points he was paid to decipher.

If there was a way to guarantee she came out happy, he'd want to ensure it as the outcome.

At ten minutes after one o'clock, Douglas detected the darkness dropping into his gut. He sat at his desk, staring at a spreadsheet, and he couldn't figure out why he'd suddenly felt empty. He'd just had a lunch full of pasta and breadsticks. And he'd spent that lunch with the woman of his dreams. They'd even found a moment to reconcile the lie he'd fed her. He should've been at peace. But as he stared at his computer screen, watching the cursor at the top of the column dedicated to "Moisture's Farms: Annual Sales Report" blinking him into a trance, he couldn't help but allow his gaze to split that cursor by the pixels.

He daydreamed about Miranda. He wanted her at the desk beside him. The fact that she was in the conference room trying to convince Angela Prince to spend money on something they didn't need or want was screwing anxiety into his mind. There was no way Angela would agree to the sale. Miranda would then exit in a huff, or a bout of sadness—Douglas didn't know her well enough to decide how she'd react—and then she'd walk out of his life forever.

The misery in his gut, he realized, was that he'd neglected to get her phone number when they were in the car together.

After such a prolific discussion about *Die Hard*, he'd forgotten to get her number. What kind of sales rep or numbers jockey was he?

Douglas knocked every blurred screen pixel back into clarity when he slapped himself on the forehead. He'd been too much of a gentleman, got too invested in winning her the meeting to realize his personal error. Because Miranda had been so focused on getting her sale, Douglas had failed to get his own.

And that was a market outcome he couldn't afford.

Opportunity or not, damp pants or not, he got up from his chair and marched toward the conference room. This could not stand. He could not take the chance that she'd leave at the exact moment he stopped paying attention to her and started paying attention to his job. With his Christmas luck, he'd drop a pencil, bend down to pick it up, and return upright to find her halfway out the door. Not worth the risk. Not if she put that big of a smile on his face, during the holidays no less. He had to go in. He had to see her. Get her number now. While there was still time.

But, of course, there was a problem with his impulsive plan.

When he'd gotten within ten feet of the conference room, former police officer and Angela's private security agent, Harvey, stepped out from behind the left plant and positioned himself between him and the door.

Harvey shook his head. The reflection in his aviator sunglasses flashed Douglas's blurred smile back at him.

"Hi," Douglas said.

The guard said nothing.

Harvey was no waif. Standing at six-foot-four, weighing probably two hundred thirty pounds, and sporting several forearm tattoos when folded over his chest, he was an impenetrable force. When Harvey got in the way, the only other option was to turn back the way you came. As Douglas nearly ran into him, flashbacks of his first-day orientation invaded his memory: *And above all, never mess with Harvey.* A few of Douglas's coworkers had the message stitched on their chair pillows.

"I just have to get a message to our visitor," Douglas said.

Harvey shook his head.

"It'll just take a minute."

Harvey said nothing.

"In and out." He snapped his fingers. "In a flash."

Harvey said nothing.

Douglas stopped himself from continuing down this path. He didn't need to plead his case any further to know Harvey would remain fixed to his position, or that pestering him about it would do little more than tick the guy off. If he wanted to enter the office's inner sanctum, he'd have to recruit someone with authority.

He'd have to ask Gordon Riche for help.

Gordon was the office's other sales manager and heir to the company chair. Although his position involved external sales and messaging, as well as building relationships with corporate clients, he still had some leverage with internal sales, so he could help Miranda if Douglas could convince him to. But that wasn't a guarantee of success. Angela would still have to agree.

Nevertheless, Douglas had to try. Miranda could've been flourishing, but she could've been floundering, and if Douglas wanted to become her hero, then he'd have to tip the outcome in her favor. So, he smiled at Harvey, tilted his head, then dashed off for reception as if he'd just committed an act of shame.

Gordon's office was in the administration and management wing of the building, opposite the sales and marketing floor where Douglas worked. In contrast to Douglas's floor, which was a drab rectangle of white walls, grey floors, and egg white dividers, diversified only by the presence of floor plants and desk trinkets, the administration and management wing was a warm tube of polished mahogany or oak, with blazing maroon rugs and framed painted landscapes. Any depression a worker felt inside his cubicle, he could zap out of existence just by entering the cozy space of the administration and management wing. Douglas knew it was a psychological trick to make him comfortable with the bosses, but he still fell for it every time he entered.

Once inside the wing, his anxiety dropped a little, and his stomach experienced a moment of peace. But not enough. Time was against him no matter his surroundings.

He jogged to the end of the hall and knocked on Gordon's door. The wooden surface was soft on his knuckles. Like punching an old desk. A tired voice answered back. Douglas opened the door.

"You have a second?" Douglas asked.

Gordon Riche, a reasonably handsome guy who had just a few years on Douglas, was too busy to look up from his desk to offer a courteous acknowledgment. He had a phone in one hand and a keyboard under the other. It looked as if the caller had him on hold. Sally, the office receptionist, was in there with him with a stack of papers clutched in her fist. She looked almost as harangued as Gordon, possibly from the documents Gordon was having her review, but also possibly from the exhausted atmosphere permeating the room.

"Angela was wondering if you could help her with a decision," Douglas said to Gordon.

Gordon closed his eyes and shook his head.

"Did she say about what?"

"She's in the conference room, trying to decide whether to buy these really useful books from this highly attractive woman, and she thinks it's a great idea, but she just needs confirmation that she's making the right call."

"Tell her I'm trying to buy the company another year of existence. She can make that decision without me."

"It would really just take a second."

Gordon glanced up from his computer screen. His face had grown even more exhausted.

"I can't help until these people get back to me. Not sure when that'll be. I'll pop in if I get a chance."

"Is it the woman from this morning?" Sally asked.

Douglas smiled at her.

Sally shifted in her seat and rolled her eyes at him.

"What?" Douglas asked.

"She's wasting her time with those books."

"You don't know that."

"When has Angela ever gone over budget?"

Douglas frowned. He was trying to stay on the side of optimism here.

"Miranda deserves to be heard. I think the books and brochures would be great for the company. Good for everyone."

"They'll litter my desk."

"Then put them on the table. Give Miranda a chance. She's worth it. I mean, they're worth it."

"Miranda?" Sally had a smirk on her face. "First name basis already?"

Douglas said nothing.

"I've noticed you staring at her since lunch time."

Douglas said nothing.

Sally turned back toward the desk and thumbed through the stack of documents in her hand. "Be careful, Doug."

"Of what?"

"Of getting your heart broken again."

"You're reading too deep into things. She just needs to be heard."

"Yeah? You think so? We need books and brochures that badly?"

"Wouldn't hurt."

"But it might hurt you if you keep thinking this way."

"What way?"

"You moped around the office for weeks when that last woman, what was her name, rejected you after the third date."

"That was Jodie, and she shoved cheesecake in my face in front of a dozen people."

"You kept talking about marriage. I swear I thought you were about to buy her a ring."

"We were hitting it off."

"*You* were hitting it off. *She* was humoring you so you would buy her web services. Talking about marriage freaked her out."

"You're crazy."

"And you saved us an expensive web service plan."

"I never bought her a ring."

"Okay, did you recycle the one you bought for the woman before her? What was her name? Becky from the phone company?"

"I never bought anyone a ring. I just liked their company."

"So much you scared them off?"

Sally knew nothing about Miranda or those other women. Such ignorant judgment.

Douglas didn't want to overplay his hand here, or continue this conversation, so he thanked Gordon for his time and shut the office door behind him.

Then he ran back to the sales and marketing floor, hoping Miranda hadn't slipped out and left while he was trying to save her sale. On his way past Sally's reception desk, he knocked over her cup of pencils. Maybe she'd spend more time picking them up than concerning herself with his business.

When he rounded the corner and passed the potted plant, he found Harvey still guarding his spot. Miranda was still inside. Douglas hadn't missed her.

Calming his breathing, Douglas returned to his desk and waited. Perhaps Gordon would appear and cast Harvey aside sooner than later. Then all would be well again.

But he needed to think of a backup plan in case Gordon didn't show up.

Chapter 5

Douglas checked over his shoulder once more, hoping to catch a glimpse of Miranda. But Harvey was in the way, standing guard at the door with his arms crossed, yawning. Or maybe roaring. Hard to tell with him.

Douglas went back to checking emails. Somewhere behind the glass, Miranda was trying to convince Angela to buy those books, probably failing. And Douglas had made it possible. Kinda.

If only he could tip the scale in her favor.

But he couldn't. He was out here. Doing his job. Like a responsible worker. No chance to rescue or assist her.

His stomach growled. Some Christmas Miracle.

After checking his latest emails, Douglas opened his project file and skimmed the data. Row after row, column after column, the numbers all looked the same. At some point, he'd have to interpret them and convert them into a data analysis sheet he could send off to the project managers who could send it off to the marketing team. At that point, they'd make new decisions with the numbers that would find their way to Angela, giving her yet another decision on top of the last decision, which could impact previous decisions that would later require new decisions. It was an endless wash cycle made dull by the tedium of featureless workdays, and Douglas had to insert himself as the laundry detergent in this continuous spin cycle of data and decisions. Or the dirty clothing. He wasn't sure of his ultimate role here. He just knew he was tired of the same old same old, and his eyes were tired of it, too.

Having Miranda in the building was the only thing making the monotony bearable. If only he could be in the conference room with her.

If only Harvey wasn't such a powerful lock on the conference room door.

He sighed. Went back to his project file. Skimmed the data. Fantasized about Miranda. Checked the clock. Only fifteen minutes had passed since they'd gotten back from lunch.

This wasn't going to work. He collapsed on his keyboard and raked his fingernails across his scalp. Douglas could be professional any other day of the year. And any other day, that would've been fine.

Today, he had to be different. Today, he had to be bold. Fearless. Innovative.

He looked over his shoulder. Harvey's arms were folded over his chest, and his eyes stared across the room at nothing. He was an unmovable sentinel, watching everything and absorbing nothing, undistracted by personal interests, and unburdened by personal thoughts. He was a human guard dog, but one who couldn't be persuaded by a dog treat, or any treat Douglas could conjure from a coworker's desk.

Getting past him would take a Christmas Miracle. Or maybe some cleverness.

He stared at his screen. Maybe the answer was in his spreadsheet. Or on YouTube. He checked the main page for the top videos of the day. A few epic fails he'd bookmark for later, but nothing about how to bypass a human wall to get to the woman of his dreams. He'd have to think of a solution himself. He raked his fingers through his hair again.

Over the next few minutes, the ideas poured through his thoughts. Most of them were terrible.

If Douglas crunched the numbers, he could find just one solution that might've worked. It was a dangerous and foolish solution, but given the prize, not exactly reckless. It gave him the one chance he needed to get to Miranda before she could sneak out and disappear from his life forever. But it could've failed miserably, too.

There was only one way to find out.

Before he got up from his chair, he took a moment to think about his will. Then he remembered he'd never written one. He frowned, remembering why he'd never written one. Whom would he give his stuff to if this plan didn't work?

With any luck, the plan would work. Then he could write a will bequeathing all his possessions to Miranda. Hopefully, she liked furniture.

He adjusted his tie, straightened his hair, and said a prayer. Then he got up from his chair. It was time to see if his hasty plan stood a chance of succeeding.

"If Angela asks, I'll tell her you're in the bathroom."

Harvey shook his head.

"Everyone's gotta go sometime, even you."

Harvey shook his head.

"You serious?"

Harvey nodded.

"Can you just look the other way for a minute?"

Harvey shook his head.

"You know you're a jerk, right?"

Harvey shrugged.

"It's Christmas. You should let me in."

Harvey shook his head.

"What if I gave you a hundred dollars?"

Harvey lowered his aviators, turned up his eyes in thought, but said nothing.

"Two hundred dollars," Douglas said.

Harvey made eye contact. Still, he said nothing.

"Three hundred?"

"A million," Harvey said, nudging his aviators back in place.

Douglas felt lightning race through his body.

"A million? You insane?"

Harvey shrugged.

"I'll move for a million. Anything less, and you can screw off."

Douglas backed off. He didn't have a million. He'd never have a million. And even if he had a million, he wouldn't give it to Harvey. Not because he thought gaining access to Miranda wasn't worth a million. It was. But because if he had a million, he wouldn't be here, and he wouldn't have met Miranda.

"Three hundred thirty," Douglas said. "That's my final offer."

Harvey blew Douglas a raspberry. "Chump change."

"It's all I have."

"Then you're a loser, and now I won't let you in on principle."

"Principle?"

"I can't in good conscience let you near our visitor when you're clearly a poor representation of our company."

"What?"

"I said—"

Douglas kicked Harvey in the groin. This was the variable he knew he'd have to play. If Harvey wouldn't play fair, then neither would he. As the big guard buckled, Douglas dodged around him. As he expected, Harvey grabbed at him as he passed but was too slow to catch him. To keep him agitated longer, Douglas backhanded him in the ear on his way past, giving him just enough time to slip into the conference room without injury.

When Douglas bolted the door shut behind him, talk about Christmas faded and everything around him went silent.

Sitting at the conference table about twelve feet away, Miranda and Angela were looking back at him. Both were tapping their fingernails at him. *Clack. Clack. Clack.* Angela's eyes then flicked at the glass door behind him. Harvey was pressing his entire body against it like a tree frog. Douglas, horrified by the sight of him, skipped away and caught himself on the side of a chair.

"I had Harvey posted there for a reason," Angela said.

"I know, but this is important," Douglas said.

Angela nodded.

"That's fine, but he's there for a reason. Please unlock the door."

"I can't. I kneed him in the groin."

Angela's face soured.

"Now, why on earth would you do a thing like that? Don't you ever read the seat cushions?"

"Because I have to talk to Miranda."

Angela glanced at their visitor. Miranda was too distracted by her books to give Douglas any attention.

"This one here comes in a pack of a hundred," she said, pushing the one in her hand across the table's surface toward Angela.

Angela pawed at the book and nodded at her. But she was more interested in the door, as her attention went back to it.

"Don't make me get out of my chair," she said. "It might change my mood. Unlock the door."

"I just—" Douglas scurried over to where Miranda was sitting. She bolted upright from his sudden presence. "Miranda, before you go—"

"We have rules around here," Angela said. "I never gave you the authority to break them. I told you not to bother us."

She got up from her chair, causing it to whine from its sudden spring of release.

"I know we just met—"

Douglas couldn't help but watch Angela from the corner of his eye. She was dashing for the door. He could feel his heart racing on two fronts now.

"But I'd very much like it if—"

"This meeting is private," Angela said. "It is not for your input."

Angela released the lock on the door. Harvey thrust it open, nearly knocking her to the side. His arms were angled like a gorilla's and his hands were balled into fists. His shoulders were leaping several inches per breath, which was coming out like an air volcano through his nose. Douglas straightened his back. Whatever he wanted to tell Miranda, he'd lost the thought. Harvey was now stomping toward him.

"Okay, before you get upset at me."

Harvey punched the palm of his hand.

"Too late for that," Harvey said.

"You have to understand this had to be done."

"I understand. Now you understand that *this* has to be done."

Douglas backed away, but he wasn't quite fast enough this time. Harvey grabbed him by the neck and cocked his fist back.

"The hell's going on in here?" came a booming voice by the door.

Harvey glanced over his shoulder, then quickly released his grip. He brushed Douglas's collar straight. Douglas peeked around Harvey's biceps. Gordon, son of the owner and the company's owner-in-waiting, was standing in the doorway with a stack of papers in hand.

"Conflict resolution training," Angela said, no shame on her face. "What can I do for you, Gordon?"

Gordon passed along the stack of papers. "Been trying to give these to you since this morning. Your pit bull there is too aggressive. Doesn't know whom to respect around here."

"I'm still teaching him. At least he's housebroken. What did you need?"

"He better be. Two things. One, I need you to review these accounts and confirm whether we're still getting commissions on them. These are the ones who aren't picking up their phones. Two, I hear you need help."

Angela shrugged. "Help with what?"

Gordon winked at Douglas, then flashed his attention at Miranda. "Who are you?"

"She's our guest," Angela said.

"What's with all the literature on the table?"

"Product management," Angela said. "I thought it would be a good idea to train our employees on how to resist outside marketers."

Miranda's shoulders deflated at the sound of that. Gordon's expression changed. Now he was studying Angela, head tilted in her favor. He looked interested in this concept, as if helping her make the sale was no longer on the table, or as if *this* was the sale always on the table.

"How's it going so far?" Gordon asked.

"Well, so far she's following the script."

"What script is that?" Miranda asked.

Angela said nothing.

Gordon, meanwhile, switched his attention to Douglas.

"Why are you here exactly?" Gordon asked. "You never quite explained it earlier. Are you part of this conversation?"

Angela crossed her arms.

"No, he's not."

Douglas said nothing.

"Then why are you here?"

Douglas tilted his head toward Miranda. He wasn't sure how to answer the question without exposing his lies—or his justified fake truths, rather—or truths left to interpretation—or his latest truth. Yeah, that one.

"That's the mystery, isn't it?" Angela said. "Won't do his work, and he won't be a team player."

He had to push back on that last one.

"I'm totally working. Just stretching my legs. And I'm absolutely a team player. For example, I'm helping Harvey learn how to become a civilized member of society."

Harvey grunted as he lurched toward Douglas's throat, but he stopped himself when Angela shook her head at him.

"But you've extricated yourself from our Christmas party," Angela said. "That's where the *team* will be this afternoon."

"I haven't extricated myself. What are you talking about?"

"Have you gotten your Secret Santa gift yet?"

"Of course." He hadn't.

She checked her watch.

"Because the party is in less than two hours, and I'd hate for you to come unprepared."

"I'm ready."

"Good. Now, answer the question. Why are you here?"

Douglas glanced at Miranda, who was wrangling all her books and other printed mockups into her bag. Clearly, the show was over. Angela had been humoring her, and now Miranda knew the truth.

"I just wanted to—"

"Because no one here invited you," Angela said.

The way Harvey was staring Douglas down, it appeared he was on Angela's side in this thinking.

"And you should go," she added.

Douglas waited to see what Miranda would do. She continued sweeping her books in her bag, but she was making no effort to stand. Maybe she would make one final plea to close her sale. Or maybe she wanted to rebuke Angela's dishonesty. Or maybe—

"Now, why are we stopping a perfectly good training session before it's finished?" Gordon asked. "Please, please. Everyone, take a seat. Given the tension in the room, I'd really like to see how you conduct your product management and conflict resolution training. It seems a bit . . . messy to me."

Angela rolled her eyes and sat down at the nearest seat alongside the conference table. Gordon took a seat beside her. Miranda finished stuffing her books in her bag and was now starting to rise, but Gordon stopped her.

"Miss, please. I never caught your name."

"What does it matter?"

"Come now. What is it?"

"Miranda."

He lowered his hands toward the table.

"I'd like you to stay, Miranda."

"I have other business to attend to. Thanks, though."

Gordon slapped his hand against the table.

"Miss! Please. Sit."

Miranda exhaled and took her seat. Douglas wanted to reach out and wrap his arm around her shoulder. But he knew that was inappropriate, so he just imagined himself comforting her. Gordon then looked at Douglas and Harvey. He pointed at the nearest chairs in front of them. They each took a seat but made sure to keep an empty one between them.

"Miss, tell me why you're here."

Miranda told Gordon about her books. Gordon nodded and smiled as he ingested her story. Angela, meanwhile, stared at her phone.

"I see. I see. How intriguing. Easy information. Yes, yes. I can see that. Sounds a bit expensive though."

"We have plans for each business's needs," Miranda said. "It really is beneficial to your growth. Being that you sell fertilizer, I'd think you folks would like some growth."

Gordon nodded. His eyes met Douglas's.

"You seem determined to help," Gordon said. "What do you think about all of this?"

"I think it sounds perfect," Douglas said. Score one brownie point with the woman.

"Why?"

Douglas leaned forward, pretending he had something to back up his support. But he had nothing. He didn't really see the point in the company buying these books. It wasn't as if anyone was coming in off the street to learn more about fertilizer.

"Well, it's all part of risk-reward," Douglas said. It was a term he'd once learned in business school. "Take a risk, earn a reward."

Gordon frowned.

"I don't buy it," he said. "There must be something in the product that matches the need of the customer. While I appreciate the gesture, I don't understand the need for this. How does this help the company?"

"Because it's thinking outside the box."

Douglas smiled. He wasn't prepared to say anything so bold and accurate, but even as it left his mouth, he knew it was the right thing to say. Gordon relaxed his shoulders and gestured Douglas to keep going. Apparently, he'd hit the right line of thinking.

"Kind of like how I kneed Harvey here in the groin," he said. Harvey grunted at this, and Douglas could tell he was clenching his fists out of the corner of his eye. But he kept going. "I had to get in this room somehow, even though he didn't want to let me in. That meant thinking outside the box. But, what's in the box, you may ask?"

"Yes, what's in the box?" Angela said, not looking up from her phone.

"A bulky man who refuses to listen to reason. When he doesn't listen to reason, then you get him to listen to your knee."

"This is absurdity," Harvey said.

"No, no," Gordon said. "I want to hear more. Tell me more about how you committed assault on my property."

Douglas felt his chest sink. That wasn't the message he was trying to tell.

"I didn't—I didn't commit assault. Hardly. I mean look at the man. That's like saying a mosquito bite is assault. No, no. I merely gestured with slight force that I wanted into the room."

"Even though you weren't invited?" Angela asked.

"Please, you weren't really interested in anything Miranda had to say, and you know it."

"Watch your tone."

Douglas took a breath.

"Okay, let me explain this another way. Imagine it's Christmas, and Harvey and you, Gordon, and, I don't know, me and some dude named Peter, I guess, are participating in a contest for a million dollars. We can assume this contest has rules."

"Peter the artist?" Gordon asked.

Douglas considered the question. There was a Peter who did something with accounts at the other end of the office. He was usually quiet and kept to himself, but whenever he'd interact with anyone, he'd say some odd things. In fact, the last time Douglas was forced to speak to him, Peter changed the subject and complained about the honeybees. Douglas walked away before Peter could finish his rant.

"Yeah, that guy," Douglas said.

Gordon rubbed his hands together.

"Good, I like that guy," he said. "This sounds like a fantastic story. Tell me more."

Douglas shrugged. Now he was committed to the tale.

He'd just have to make sure not to present himself as too special or Peter too unremarkable. Whenever he wanted to convince management of anything, the first thing he had to do was humble himself. So, he'd make himself humble.

Christmas Log

LATE LAST NOVEMBER, a local radio show hosted a contest where people could win a million dollars if they participated in a simple game for Christmas. The station offered no rules or guidelines, nor did it post any disclaimers or describe any details about the game. It simply announced on the morning of Black Friday that anyone who called before 10 a.m. would be eligible to enter the contest, and that details would be given the day it began. In fact, the only stipulations it had added before soliciting for callers were:

1. The station had the right to pick whomever it wanted to participate without explanation.

2. Anyone who called for eligibility was committed to enter upon acceptance on the contest's start date.

3. Selected participants had to be available to play the game on Christmas morning.

4. The contest would be held in a facility designated by the station.

5. Whoever won the contest would be given a million dollars, tax-free, on the spot.

By 10:01 that morning, the radio station had fielded more than ten thousand callers.

It narrowed the field by factors known only to its psychology team and ended up selecting four single men: Peter, the reclusive art student, Douglas, the depressed businessman, Harvey, the angry police officer, and Gordon, the ambitious sales manager. When the station psychologist called each of them to confirm the station's selection, he verified each detail they had given him during the screening process. The psychologist wrote the following on his profile sheet:

PETER: Enjoys being alone most days. Studying art at the university but is thinking about dropping out to focus entirely on his paintings. Never sold any of his art. Known for being quiet and in no one's way. Tends to skip parties. Isn't usually invited to parties.

DOUGLAS: Recently laid off from his job managing accounts for lawyers. Trying to get work at a new firm, but no one is hiring. Divorced, no children. Spends most days in front of the television. Doesn't know what else to do with his life.

HARVEY: Adrenaline junkie who likes to pick fights. Often reprimanded at his job for causing trouble just to feel alive. Dates often but can't commit to anyone. Hates kids. Has been fired for insubordination at nearly every job he's worked. Threatens his suspects with violence if they don't confess to their crimes within ten minutes—he likes things done on his schedule, not theirs.

GORDON: Generally optimistic person who gets along with almost anyone. He seeks opportunities wherever available and always knocks, even when the door is closed and locked. Often considered for promotions; passed up only when he hasn't finished building up a required skill, which he's always working on. Takes good care of himself. Unmarried, only because he doesn't want to hurt a woman's feelings by accident.

On the day of the contest, the four men were sent a text message with the time and address at which to show up. They were instructed to arrive at a building about two blocks from the station by noon. Gordon and Harvey arrived early. Douglas came dragging his feet through the door just after twelve. Peter overslept that morning and didn't check his phone until 11:30. He arrived just after 1:00. Harvey pushed him against the wall and held his elbow over his chest for making them all start so late.

"Now, now," the host said, when he watched Harvey react to Peter's tardiness. "This is no time to fight. Everyone's here now, so we can begin. Please take a seat."

The four men were standing in a room made of gray walls and a black floor, completely empty, save for the row of plastic chairs arranged together at the center. They glanced at each other and shrugged, then shuffled to the middle of the floor. Each man took a seat and waited for further instructions. The host left the room.

"Hey, where you going, pal?" Harvey yelled at the host's back. Harvey's echo answered him instead.

"Must be part of the game," Gordon said. "How fun and mysterious."

Harvey glared at him. Clearly the host was wasting their time.

The host was actually making them wait while he searched for the person who was in charge of the game. When he returned about twenty minutes later, he brought an older gentleman back with him. Everyone but Gordon was fidgeting by the time he reentered the room.

"This is Doctor Reever," the host said. "He is the person responsible for designing this game. He will give you instructions on how to play in just a moment. Now, if you'll each follow me."

The four men got out of their chairs and followed the host down a dark corridor. At the end of the corridor was an adjacent hall. At either end of the adjacent hall was a door made of iron. Just beyond each door was a turn down yet another hallway. Both doors had a security guard stationed beside it.

The host stopped them at the T-junction at the end of the main hall.

"Behind me is a ballroom divided into four quadrants. Each quadrant has a steel wall on all four sides and an iron door separating them from the outside hall. You will each choose a room to call your own. Then you will await further instructions."

The four men exchanged looks. They weren't sure exactly what this game was about. They knew only that they were committed to play it, per the rules, and that the prize for winning was a million dollars. So, they were nervously excited and couldn't wait to begin. But they didn't know *what* they were excited to begin.

Peter and Douglas each took the rooms connected to the front hallway; Harvey and Gordon took the ones in the back. Only Gordon made eye contact with his respective guard as he entered. Each guard closed and locked the iron doors behind them.

"Each room is the same," Dr. Reever said through an intercom in the ceiling. "Please take a moment to examine your surroundings."

The men did as they were told.

They were each enclosed in a private square room about forty-by-forty feet. The rooms had slightly convex floors, with concentric layers of Christmas trees circling a fallen log and a plastic chair in the middle. On two separate ends of each room, a wooden table stood beside the wall. A box of matches, a box of cigarettes, a pencil, and a hacksaw were sitting on the tables nearest to the doors. Five boxes of crackers, three gallons of water, and a paper cup were sitting on the tables at the other end of each room. Some of the trees had lights strung around them, but none had ornaments. Three trees in each room had a present underneath, each wrapped in different colored wrapping paper. A drain sat in the middle of each floor under the plastic chairs. A cracked pipe ran the length of each ceiling directly over the chairs. The ceilings were about twelve feet high. Four halogen lamps hung from each ceiling equidistant from each other, about ten feet from each center of the rooms.

"When you're done looking at your surroundings, please take a seat," Dr. Reever said.

Each man sat on his chair for nearly five minutes before the psychologist spoke again.

"Now, the game is simple. In the middle of your room, next to your chair, you will see a log lying on the floor. Somewhere in that log is a metal key. That key will unlock your door. The first person to walk through his door will win a million dollars. The second to walk through his door will win twenty thousand dollars and a free trip to Europe. The third to walk through his door will win a free dinner for two at the restaurant of his choice. The fourth to leave will go home empty-handed as a disgrace to his people. You have what you need to get to that key. The first to get his door open will be a millionaire. It's that simple. Good luck, gentlemen.

"Begin."

As soon as the psychologist's voice died out, a drop of water bubbled up and fell from the crack in the ceiling pipe. Another drop fell a few seconds later.

It would drip indefinitely.

This was the moment the game would become real to them.

Peter

Because he was used to spending his days alone, Peter did not see a problem here. In fact, he already saw himself at an advantage over the others because they were likely to go crazy from isolation if this project were to take them too long, a condition he was already well practiced with. And that was also an advantage for him because he could see this as a project and not as a competition. Any project worth its salt required time to perfect, and this was something he could see taking time. The trick, of course, was to figure out what his vision was, both for the tree log, and for the goal of getting out. Because art took time, the idea of ripping the log to pieces, grabbing the key, and racing out of here first was practically barbaric. He would not do the project justice. And, because as an artist he was conditioned to expect very little pay for his effort, he had already gotten the illusion out of his head that he would be the winner of a million dollars. He figured he could settle for the twenty thousand, or even the free dinner, which was a fair price for designing an art project made of wood.

Douglas

As a former killer in the business world, Douglas knew the value of money and the power it held sway over anyone's motivation to succeed at his goals. But his job was to convince others to buy stuff they didn't need, to trust lawyers who might screw them later, and it was a job he had lost due to a change in the market's expectations of him. If he could lose his position so easily, then he wasn't sure he even deserved the money. He wanted it, sure. The same ingredient that had convinced him to give the business world a try was the same ingredient that got him to call the radio station and join this silly contest in the first place. But life was passing him by so quickly. Other competitors, younger, faster, stronger, were coming up the line behind him and outshining him at every turn. He figured the same would happen here. No matter how hard he'd fight to get to that key, his three rivals would undoubtedly get to it first. They'd be faster, smarter, or even luckier than he was. He'd be the big loser in this contest no matter how hard he tried, and he knew it. So, he kept to his chair and stared at the log, trying to decide just how much effort he should put into this, if any.

Harvey

Criminals feared no one in the police force as much as they feared Harvey, for he was a veteran at using his surroundings to his advantage. He'd take the bad guys down by throwing trashcan lids at their heads or rolling bowling balls at their feet. He'd draw his firearm on an old lady jaywalking if he thought it would scare her out of ever breaking the law again. He also had his fair share of suspensions over the years, thanks to his occasional need to shoot someone in the knee for a lack of cooperation. All in the name of justice, of course. Even though he pissed off everyone he'd met at some point or another, he did so because it got the job done. And getting the job done was the most important thing in life to him, no matter what ends he'd have to make meet to accomplish it. It was important in life, important in business, and it was important here in this cell full of Christmas trees. And to get the job done meant getting to that key before anyone else could even catch a whiff of it. So, he would have to use his resources to the best of his ability. That much he knew for certain.

Peter

The number one job of an artist is to create a masterpiece, and no masterpiece can be completed without the right tools. Because he had explored the room prior to the psychologist's announcement, Peter already had an idea about what he needed to get the job done. So, he went to the table at the far end to get a drink of water and a quick snack of crackers. He knew he had a long night ahead of him, so he got his fill now so he could concentrate on the project without further distraction from things like hunger or thirst.

Once he was satisfied, he circled the room to the other table and grabbed the hacksaw. Even though he didn't want to cut the log into tiny pieces, he did want to whittle some of it down, to shape it into something elegant. What he thought he could do was to carve an ornamental canoe out of it.

He kicked the plastic chair out of the way and knelt beside the log. With his only obstacle removed, he began scraping the hacksaw across the log's bark surface to unearth the beautiful boat inside.

Already, though, he sensed a problem. During his initial scouting period, he had forgotten to check the properties of both the log and the hacksaw, so he failed to realize how much of an upward battle he would have to fight.

The log was made from a fallen mahogany tree, not a traditional Christmas pine. So, the bark was tough. Very tough. Not impossible to cut, of course, for someone had managed to chop it into a log, and, according to Dr. Reever, to insert a key into the trunk somehow. But still, very difficult, and ultimately very strenuous and time-consuming to whittle down any part of it, and even more tiresome to search for the key. He would likely have to make a few adjustments to his vision to keep from tiring out completely.

The other problem was with the hacksaw. In short, no one had sharpened it prior to leaving it on the table. Even as he took the first swipe of the blade across the log's surface, he barely nicked the wood. It was hardly better than using a butter knife to cut it. The job would take him much longer to complete than he had anticipated.

He brought the three jugs of water to the center of the room to keep himself hydrated while he embarked on the creative process.

Douglas

As a businessman, Douglas was used to making profitable deals. It was how he survived into his thirties. But here in this lonely room, he had no one to haggle with, no one to offer him feedback regarding his success, and no one to urge him to try harder if things weren't looking bright. All he had was his own drive, his own wit, and the limited tools his company had offered him—the radio station being the company in this case—and the ensuing combination of all three elements did not add up to anything powerful. In short, his chances of success were minimal, just as they had been in the dying days of his career, and more personally, his marriage.

He knew the problem he was facing. There was a key somewhere in the heart of this thick, possibly impenetrable mahogany log. He could maybe dig for it with his fingernails. But that would've hurt, causing his fingertips to burst with blood. He also thought about using the hacksaw to cut the log into pieces, but the blade was so dull that he would've been lucky to even shave it, and using it would've caused him so much fatigue, and he was already fatigued with life. Granted, he didn't see any other option here. If he wanted to get to the center of the log, he'd have to get his hands dirty. That was just the way it had to be. In his line of work, he was used to others getting their hands dirty on his behalf.

He didn't know which way to go from here, so he plucked a cigarette from the pack on the table near the door, struck a match, lit the filter, stubbed the match onto the concrete floor, and returned to the chair as he waited for his nerves to calm.

Then he had an idea.

At first, he was surprised by his originality, but then he thought about how business worked. Everything in life requires supply and demand. When he managed accounts for lawyers, he had to supply the paperwork his employers demanded. When the evidence they demanded couldn't be found, he'd supply it by giving them a substitute truth. There was always a method for getting things done according to need, even if the method required a little bit of cheating.

In this case, Douglas thought the best way to get to the center of the log was to dull the wood first. So, he pushed the chair out of the way, then rolled the log under the pipe drip, and then sat back in the chair and waited for the water to erode the wood. He even helped it along by dumping two of his three gallons of water all over it.

Now he had to sit there and wait for the wood to rot. Then he could start hacking it to pieces.

While he sat there, staring at the log, he thought about all the things he had lost in the name of doing what he thought was right for his career. He began to cry.

Harvey

As a man who couldn't be bothered with wasting time, Harvey went right to work the moment Dr. Reever went off the air, looking for any resource he could find to pulverize that tree as quickly as possible. He put guys away in prison all the time, and he hated the feeling of being locked up himself. The sooner he got out of this hellhole, the better.

He knew what resources the tables had to offer, but he didn't know what was inside the three gifts he had found under the Christmas trees in the concentric circles around him. So, he gathered each of the presents, brought them to the table with the hacksaw, and tore into them. He found a pile of coal in one of the boxes, a bell in another, and a package of beef jerky in the third. None of these were helpful.

Then he took the hacksaw and gnawed at the tree bark with its dull blade. He feverishly tore into it for five minutes before his arm went into a spasm and he found himself out of breath. On his moment of rest, he jogged to the water table, poured himself a drink, chugged it down in a single gulp, then went back to work on the log. He spent another five minutes trying to cut into the surface of its mahogany hide. When he fell back panting, he saw he had dug into it by only half an inch. And that was just one groove. The log was about two feet thick in diameter, about five feet long, and the hole that had been cut out to hide the key had been filled in so well that he couldn't detect where someone had tampered with it. It would take him days to find it at this rate. Maybe weeks.

Frustrated with his new reality, he took the chair and began hammering it against the log, hoping to take out bigger chunks of wood. The tremors associated with impact rumbled all the way down through his wrists and elbows and up into his shoulders, and he nearly lost his balance, but he kept whacking at it, kept hoping to make that precious dent in its surface. The chair broke on the third hit. He started kicking it with his foot instead. He broke that, too.

Then the most genius of ideas came to him. It was the idea that would make him the guaranteed winner of the contest. In fact, he was so certain of its success that he laughed at himself for not seeing it before, when he wasn't crying from the pain in his foot. This was clearly the way the game's designers had intended for him to win. They didn't want to reward patience; they wanted to reward intelligence. He laughed at himself again for being such a fool. A fool until now.

Harvey hobbled up to the table by the door and grabbed the pile of coal. Then he brought the coals to the log and lined them up against its curved underside. Then he dragged several Christmas trees to the log and tipped them over in a crisscross pattern. Then he took the box of matches and set the whole thing ablaze.

He waited for the log to burn into a pile of ash. His goal was to let the key come to him.

Unfortunately, because the kindling extended to the innermost ring of trees, the fire had no trouble jumping to a new surface, and it spread to each concentric circle of Christmas trees within minutes. Harvey passed out from heat and smoke inhalation before he could discover whether his plan would even work.

Gordon

As soon as the lingering resonance of Dr. Reever's voice faded out, Gordon considered the situation he was in, considered the money and freedom he wanted, and sought the most obvious method for getting out. He knew the game he was playing. He figured his competitors were already hard at work trying to get to that key. And he knew he should do everything he could to also get to that key.

The issue was that the psychologist had never told them to use the key outright. He told them only that it was there, and that their job was to be the first to escape the room.

So, instead of wasting his time trying to dig for the key, he simply went to the door and asked the guard to let him out.

"Seriously?" the guard asked.

"The rules didn't say I couldn't ask," Gordon said. "So, I'm exercising my right to think outside the box."

The guard was looking at him through the tiny, barred window, incredulous, but intrigued at the same time. Gordon could see the hesitation in his eyes, so he helped him out.

"We can do things for ourselves any time," Gordon said. "But we do things better as a team, do we not?"

The guard shrugged.

"Makes sense."

"And we have not because we ask not, right?"

"I've heard that somewhere, yeah."

"So, this isn't prison. You're not under any obligation to keep me locked up here. And if you are, no one here has made that clear to me. So, the way I see it, you have to let me out because I'm asking you to let me out."

"Makes sense, but—"

"And you can't legally hold me here because I didn't sign any form or contract that explains you can, or should. The only contract I signed was the one explaining to me that I had to abide by the rules of the game, and that by winning the game, I would win a million dollars.

"The rules state that I must get out of here. The rules do not restrict my method of getting out. The rules do not state that I must hold a key in hand. The rules only state that I must walk through my door before anyone else walks through his door to win the prize. So, unless you'd like to be sued for breach of contract or holding me here against my will, please open this door."

The guard shrugged.

"All right, fair enough."

And so, the guard opened the door for Gordon, and Gordon walked through with his chin held high, and he tipped his head in gratitude to the man who had given him freedom and, ultimately, the win.

"For your help," he said, "I'll give you a small cut. How's a hundred thousand-dollar Christmas bonus sound to you?"

The guard smiled.

"Sounds real good, sir. Real good."

"Good. You help me, I help you. I'll put that in writing if you'd like."

Later that night, the psychologist awarded Gordon his million-dollar paycheck, and Gordon used the money to better himself, better his investments, and better those in need around him. He also gave the guard the cut he had promised him, which was good because the guard had a new baby on the way and really could've used the help.

Peter, the artist, earned his twenty thousand dollars and trip to Europe five days later, when he managed to scoop the key out from the log after carving fourteen inches down near the head of the canoe, while forming what would've become a seat and footwell. He abandoned his project when he realized he could make something better using better tools, which he could now buy thanks to his twenty-thousand-dollar payoff. He also resolved to pitch his next project to museum curators when he was ready to visit the Louvre.

Douglas, the depressed businessman, earned his free dinner-for-two a week and a half later, when he finally decided that waiting for the log to erode was foolish, and that he was better off hacking the thing to pieces. Because he took action several days after everyone else had started, he was too far behind to catch up. But his growing thirst from having only one gallon of water left was enough to knock him out of his stupor, and he was diligent after that. As soon as he found the key, he realized all he needed this whole time was just a little push.

Now that he had it, he thought he'd use his free dinner-for-two as an opportunity to impress a new business connection and hopefully rise out of his funk. He stole the pencil from the table to commemorate the moment he had embraced his newfound spark. Maybe he could sign a deal with it.

Harvey, the angry police officer, was carried out of his cell and put on life support about twenty minutes after he'd passed out. Because the rules did state that he had to walk out of the room, not get carried out, he had to forfeit his second-place prize to the next person who did walk out on his own two feet. The rules had also forgone any mention of liability in the case of injury, so Harvey was left responsible for his own medical bills, which included treatment for smoke inhalation and third-degree burns. He later lost his job for having been away for so long, and for basically being physically unfit to continue. The fire he'd started managed to char the log and burn the needles off every tree in the room, but it did not reduce any of it to cinders like he had hoped. However, when facility workers came in to extinguish the fire, they cut the remains of the log open to find that the metal key had melted from intense heat. The radio station decided to bill Harvey for damages. It also had to report the incident to the authorities as possible arson and endangerment to others, to cover its own butt from liability. Harvey's legal future remains in question to this day.

Chapter 6

WHEN DOUGLAS FINISHED THE story, Harvey was fuming, and Gordon was gleaming.

"I always knew I'd win," Gordon said. He rubbed the corner of his eye. "So good."

"Yeah, tough luck about your loss," Angela said. "Based on a true story?"

Douglas said nothing. If she was a Christmas elf, then she was a dark Christmas elf.

Gordon, meanwhile, slapped his palm against the table. "Well, I see your point. Maybe we shouldn't dismiss this idea so quickly." He glanced at Miranda. "Miss, would you like to pitch *me* your books? Again? I do have some sway with the owner, and I happen to have a few minutes before I can call our next client. Given Mr. McCray's insights, I'm willing to listen more carefully this time. Maybe we could still find a use for these."

Miranda's eyes lit up. She straightened her back. Before saying a word, she reached into her bag and dealt her paperback mockups like a deck of cards. Gordon snatched them out of trajectory like a bear trying to catch a flying fish.

"These look nice," he said. Then he nodded at the others. "You can all go now. I'll take it from here."

Douglas sensed the conference room closing in on him the moment he made eye contact with Harvey. Even though he'd bought some time with Miranda, potentially, he had little time left before Angela's bodyguard would lose his cool. The big man's shoulders were already heaving half a foot with each angry breath. He'd angered the bull, and the red was now burned into its eyes. No matter how much time he'd bought with Miranda, it wouldn't have mattered much if he'd entered the hospital before she exited the conference room.

The simple solution would have been to stay. But Gordon had made his decree. And while Angela could be defied during her season of "Christmas spirit," especially if Douglas invoked the name of "Secret Santa" into the conversation, Gordon failed to tolerate insubordination at any time of the year. This was evident as Angela gathered her things and got up from her chair. Even she had to obey the order to vacate the conference room, if Gordon was the one who'd placed it.

As Harvey rose from his own seat and turned his sneer at Douglas into a twisted smile, Douglas recognized the danger he was in and tried to play one more card of his own to save his skin long enough for Harvey's anger to blow over.

"Say, Gordon," he said. "You're not a fan of assault on your property, right?"

Gordon nodded.

"Then would you mind keeping Harvey in here? For security purposes? Because I'm pretty sure he wants to punch my lights out."

Gordon glanced at the big, smoldering security guard. Harvey was standing over his seat, shifting his feet to the side as if to move away from the table. But he stopped. Eye contact with Gordon froze him in place. His elbows tightened, as if he was preparing to lower himself. But he hadn't fully committed to the move.

Gordon pointed his index finger down at the table. Harvey glanced at Douglas. Douglas smiled back. Harvey grunted, then looked at Gordon. Gordon jabbed his finger to the table.

Harvey sat back down. The other thing Douglas's coworkers always said was, *If you do mess with Harvey, then hide for an hour until he cools down. Next encounter will be as if nothing ever happened.*

Douglas still hadn't gotten Miranda's number, but at least Gordon had bought him time. As he reached for the door handle, he listened to Miranda's opening lines.

"So, I take it you like a good Christmas story," she said to Gordon.

"I do," Gordon said.

"Then let me tell you another. Have you heard the story about the business that sat along the shore where Christmas Pond connected to Thanksgiving Lake?"

"No."

"Okay, well listen up, because the ending may change your life."

"I'm listening."

"It starts with a boy who had a dream."

Douglas smiled as he walked out of the conference room. Sounded like the kind of story that would keep her around for at least an hour. Maybe two. Maybe she'd even stick around for the party later.

Something smacked him from the side. A stack of papers.

Angela dropped the stack Gordon had handed her in Douglas's hands.

"Since you're so keen to do a manager's job, you can start with these," she said. "If you start now, you might still make the party. If you even care."

Before Douglas could respond or protest, Angela turned her back on him and sashayed off to the reception area, where she'd ultimately head off to her office for some other activity.

<h1 style="text-align:center">Chapter 7</h1>

Almost two hours had passed when Angela ordered everyone into the office rec center, which was a small room at the rear of the building where they'd normally kept their spare supplies and a pool table with its felt surface torn near the back corner pocket. The room had been converted into a party space, with folding chairs arranged along every wall, and red and green streamers cascading down from the runners holding the panels in place. A plastic tabletop tree sat in the middle of the pool table, and everyone's Secret Santa gifts were laid in concentric rows around it. Most of them were small and took up hardly any space. A few billiards filled in the gaps, making the pile seem larger than it was.

When Douglas entered the room, he smiled. Just off to the side, near the door, Miranda was sitting between Gordon and Angela. She was jutting partially out of her seat, leaning at an angle as she held one of her books open by the spine, drawing her finger along the contents inside. Gordon nodded thoughtfully at whatever she was showing him and tracked along with her finger down the page.

Douglas slipped past them and took the nearest empty seat four chairs down, just inside the corner. The room was big enough to hold a dozen people comfortably, so he had to squeeze in to fit between Larry the accountant and Zelda the office nurse (she was actually the purchasing manager for supplies, but she was also the only one who had access to the office medical kit). But it was fine. He had a clear view of Miranda's face since she was angled enough in her chair to look right at him.

Then he realized he was holding something in his hand, the wad of box tissues containing his Secret Santa gift. He tossed it onto the table a few inches short of the nearest circle. It hit the table with a thud, and a few sheets of nose wipes shed from it. Some people, including Winston, noticed the chunky, metallic thump. After the bag rolled a quarter circle, the onlookers resumed their private discussions. Winston held his gaze on the bag a few seconds longer.

"We had cake," Angela said to the guests, as everyone resumed their poses. Except for two people—John, the office plumber (accounting assistant who also kept the key for the lock on the office plunger), and Terrance, the office deadbeat (actual title, as far as Douglas knew)—all thirty staff members were present, plus Miranda, and all thirty, minus two, plus Miranda cheered. "But Harvey deemed it unsafe, so he threw it out. Hope everyone likes peppermint."

Angela reached in her handbag and produced a gift-sized package of breath mints. The entire room grumbled. Both walls joining at an angle behind Douglas's shoulders vibrated from the noise.

"Come on, team. We can make a jolly time out of anything," Angela said. Her hands clutched her knees as she spoke, but her eyes made split-second contact with everyone's face. "That's an order."

She got out of her chair and marched to the adjacent corner, where a small table and an adorning radio sat. She pressed the radio switch, releasing the canned Christmas music she must've known was coming. Gordon, who shook his head at the radio, got up and slipped out the door. Not his type of music, probably.

"Just kidding," Angela said, as her eyes followed Gordon out the door. "I also made cookies. Peppermint caramel." She opened the supply cabinet where all the pens were kept and removed a plate covered in foil. "Everyone, take one."

She set the plate on the pool table and uncovered it. Several dozen burnt cookies were stacked and crumbling on a small pile. No one moved toward it. Angela's face soured as she scanned the room for takers.

"Eat the cookies!" she said.

A few people leaned out of their seats and pawed around for their favorites. Each was hesitant to put the cookies in their mouths. Others took the wait-and-see approach. Douglas remained fixed to his chair.

"We also have a bottle of champagne around here somewhere," Angela said, searching a small circular space around her. "Might still be on my desk if anyone wants to check."

Niles, the office sailor (offsite sales representative and former seaman), leapt out of his seat and raced for the door. Angela called after him to remind him to pick up some wine glasses out of her cabinet while he was in there.

Miranda, meanwhile, closed the book and placed it atop the stack at her feet. She slid to the edge of her seat, reaching down for the bottom stack. Her purse strap, meanwhile, shuffled over her shoulder. A wave of her hair followed.

She was positioning herself to leave.

"Hey, where you going?" Douglas demanded.

Miranda snapped her attention his way. She made eye contact, but her face was flushed. Must not have expected anyone to notice.

"I don't want to interrupt the party," she said. "Not really my place, you know?"

Douglas leaned forward to show his interest.

"This party is better with you here. You should stay."

Larry and that weird guy with the plastic doll haircut and freckles to match were watching the exchange. Douglas glared at each of them. Larry glared back, but the weird guy dodged. Larry, catching Douglas's nonverbal cue, elbowed the weird guy in the rib, then pointed at Angela, who was now dancing with her arms swaying over her head. Miranda noticed the exchange and smiled.

"I really don't belong," she said.

Douglas slid closer to the edge of his seat. He wanted to get as close to her as the two chuckleheads sitting between them would allow.

"Neither do I," Douglas said. "Yet, here we are."

Miranda held her gaze with him. Douglas fixed his gaze at her.

Then the music stopped.

"Time for presents," Angela said.

Already? Douglas thought. He checked his watch. 3:03. This was going to be the shortest party ever.

"We've got a hat somewhere around here." Angela sifted through the box of pencils beside the radio. Then she checked under the table. Douglas noticed it sitting atop the tree, but he said nothing about it. The longer the party lasted, the longer Miranda would stay.

"It's right there," Winston said. He was pointing at the tree. *Bah humbug!*

Douglas watched Miranda's feet. They weren't moving toward the door, so that was good. But her toes were tapping, despite the music going silent. Not so good. Angela, meanwhile, slipped through the narrow passage between the chairs and the pool table and reached for the top of the tree. Without wasting a moment, she tipped the bag over and dumped all the scraps of paper containing names next to the side pocket. She plucked one from the top.

"Harvey." She studied the scrap. Glanced at the door. "Why's Harvey's name in here?"

She crushed the slip of paper in her hand and dumped it down the side pocket. Reached for the next one. "Gordon."

Gordon had also left, but Angela didn't destroy it. She just set it aside for safekeeping. Next one.

"Lena."

"Yes!" The middle-aged party planner (chief accounts liaison) jumped up from her seat and chicken-walked around the table to take her name. Then she searched through the pile of gifts to find the one addressed to her. She found it near the base and showed it to the group. It had a small, skinny shape and was wrapped in dried tea leaves. Probably lipstick. "I don't know who got this for me, but—"

"I did," Johnson, the custodian (custodian) said, raising his hand.

"But thanks," Lena finished her sentence. Her grin was almost as big as her head. She didn't need any more lipstick.

"We're supposed to keep the gifts secret," Angela said, glaring at Johnson. He shrugged at her.

Lena, meanwhile, tore the tea leaves off her gift, revealing what looked like a flash drive. Made of platinum. Lena's fingers went up to her chest.

"Oh my."

"You're always complaining about losing your files," Johnson said. "So, I hope this helps."

Lena had no words. She stared at him with a grateful smile.

Even Douglas had to admit that was pretty cool of Johnson, especially on his salary.

"Very nice, Johnson," Angela said. "Okay, let's see who's next."

"You can use the wrapping to make tea," Johnson said.

Lena's head wafted back and forth, still in disbelief. "I will." Angela was calling the next name before Lena realized she had to pick up the tea leaves to use them.

Zelda was next, getting a gold watch from Larry, then Freddy the stalker (mailroom attendant), getting binoculars from Steven (Douglas didn't know his position), apparently as part of an inside joke. Then Winston got a bag of candy canes from Harvey, according to the office spy, also Freddy. Terrance was next.

But Terrance still hadn't come back from the Olive Farm. Everyone exchanged glances as if to make sure he wasn't sitting beside them.

"Where the hell is he?" Angela asked. "Doesn't he know this is the most important office event of the *entire* year?" Everyone shrugged. Having no satisfying answer, Angela set it aside. "Maybe if he decides to come back." She read the next name.

She'd gone through almost twenty names when she finally called Douglas to the table. Once she called on him, he smiled at Miranda, who was now watching him, and tiptoed toward her, reaching to his left to pluck the nearest gift from the dissolving row. He showed it to her. Then he looked at it himself. It was a rectangular box addressed to Sally, the receptionist. He put the box back and searched for the one with his name on it. Found it on the other side of the tree. It was the size of a card, and it came in an envelope.

He waved it at the group.

"Yep, just what I always wanted. A card," he said. "Love that Hallmark." But he still hated that channel.

He walked back to his seat. So, that's what his coworkers thought of him. Lena gets a flash drive. Zelda gets a watch. Even that weirdo who was sitting next to Larry gets a pair of binoculars. Douglas gets a card.

"Aren't you going to open it?" Winston asked.

"Seems personal, doesn't it?" Douglas responded.

Winston shrugged. "Might still be nice."

Everyone who was even mildly interested in this gift exchange was now staring at Douglas. He didn't know why. It was just a card. Nothing to see here.

"Maybe when I get home."

"Just open it," Angela said. "Get in the Christmas spirit. Sheesh."

"It's a card. What do I need to show it off for?" He glanced at Winston. "Thank you, if you're the one who sent it."

Winston offered Douglas a nod, neither hostile nor friendly. Safe response. Anyone who missed it would've been left to wonder who'd given him the card. Playing the game the right way.

Miranda, meanwhile, was watching the exchange. When Douglas glanced back her way, he noticed that she, too, was neither hostile nor friendly.

Maybe he should open the card.

Or maybe he should stick to his message. Not every gift is great. Only what befits the receiver. Lena deserved her flash drive. As hard of a job as tracking and sharing accounts might be, having a place to keep them all organized was thoughtful and proper. Zelda might've deserved the watch, or maybe not, but Larry was a generous guy who could afford to offer something so extravagant. Made perfect sense. Terrance didn't deserve anything, of course, but he was getting a stapler, so Douglas was being extra thoughtful in giving him a gift. But Winston giving Douglas a card? Just seemed disrespectful.

"The point of this party is to show off everyone's gratitude," Angela said. "If we didn't care about that, then we'd all just go home early."

If not for Miranda sticking around, Douglas would've been happy to go home early, but he didn't dare tell Angela that, not while her "holiday spirit" was slipping.

"Maybe I'd rather read the card in private?" Douglas didn't care where he'd read it, but he wanted this conversation to end.

Angela glared at him for so long that he forced himself to look away. She was attractive enough, but not when she stared at him like that. Miranda, meanwhile, was checking her phone.

"Let's see who's next," Angela said. Douglas could still feel the ice of her gaze sticking to the back of his neck. "Gina."

The gift exchange went on for a few more minutes, eliciting reasonably joyful responses from each recipient, especially from those who ate the cookies. For the most part, everyone got what they wanted, and they thanked their "Secret Santa" to their face. Larry played it cool when he opened his package to find a bottle of fungus remover, but that was what Larry always did. He was just a cool guy. A cool guy who was now the owner of fungus remover.

When they got down to the last two gifts, the one belonging to Gordon and the other belonging to Terrance, Angela checked the room again.

"Terrance still isn't here," she said, "and we can't let his gift sit here unattended. Anyone want it?"

A few people exchanged glances with each other the same way two people deciding who takes the last piece of cake exchange glances, but they didn't speak up. When no one volunteered, Angela nodded at Miranda.

"You don't have a gift. You want it?"

Miranda shrugged.

"I don't work here. Is that a problem?"

"Did you sell your books?"

"Not sure."

"Then take the gift. As a consolation. Just in case. It's Christmas."

"Sure, if that's okay with whoever brought it."

Douglas said nothing. Miranda deserved much better than a stapler. The less he shared about where and whom it came from, the better.

"Douglas?" Angela said. "Can Miranda have your gift to Terrance?"

Douglas lurched in his chair.

"What makes you think it's mine?"

"You're the only one who hasn't been outed yet."

He cursed under his breath. Of course that was true.

"Well, I mean . . ."

"You can have it," Angela said.

"I didn't say yes," Douglas said.

Angela lowered her gaze at him.

"I kinda think you did."

"I don't want to stir up any controversy," Miranda said.

Angela plucked the heavy wad of tissue paper off the pool table and dropped it in Miranda's hands.

"No controversy. It's yours."

"Well, if there's no objection."

Miranda took care as she lifted each sheet of tissue paper off the wad. Little by little, the black metal skin of Winston's stapler revealed itself. Like an onion, the wrapping peeled away, revealing its mechanical heart. As the last piece of tissue paper fell to the floor, Miranda was left holding the device in her hand the way Hamlet might hold a skull.

"It's nice," she said.

She glanced at Douglas and nodded, neither hostile nor friendly.

"Hey, that looks familiar," Winston said. Everyone looked his way. "Just like the one that went missing from my desk after lunch."

All eyes fell on Douglas.

"What are you all looking at me for? It's a stapler. Just like Winston's. Just like all staplers. No conspiracy theories needed here. They're all the same. Including that one."

Once again, Angela gave him that level gaze. "Is that Winston's stapler?"

Douglas shifted in his seat. He didn't understand the interrogation here. Did they want him to bring a Christmas present or not?

"You're casting unfair judgment—"

"Is that his stapler or not?" Angela crossed her arms over her chest. Her holiday cheer had already fled the building, but now her face was turning to stone. Soon it would become a gargoyle.

"My initials are on the bottom," Winston said.

Miranda flipped the stapler over. "W. F."

Douglas rolled his eyes. How did he miss checking the underside of his gift to Terrance for Winston's initials? No sense in pretending now. The more he suppressed the truth, the more he'd look like a douche to Miranda, and he'd already checked that box today. Maybe twice.

"I'll buy him a new one. Sheesh. He won't need it during the holidays."

Angela shook her head. "Do you not know anything about the meaning of Christmas?"

"Besides the fact that none of you do, either? No."

Angela sat on the pool table and adjusted her skirt to cover her knees. Then she straightened her back and challenged him.

"You know, you'd make Santa Claus a killing in the coal industry."

Douglas, remembering his Christmas card from his landlady this morning, straightened his back and retorted.

"Santa's not into coal. He's into woodwork. And abusing elves. Get your history straight."

A smile crept over Angela's lips. Everyone else in the room was oscillating their focus between them.

"You know the history of Santa Claus?" Angela asked. "You?"

"I know a version of it, yeah. I know the one that none of you ever talk about."

"Santa has more than one version?"

"Hey, are you referring to the legend of Krampus?" that guy with the binoculars asked.

Douglas had no idea what he was talking about.

"No, I'm referring to Saint Nick the bodybuilder."

The attention volley stopped. Now everyone was fixed on Douglas.

"Saint Nick *the bodybuilder?*" Angela said. "What on earth are you referring to?"

Douglas shook his head. He couldn't believe these people had never heard of the *true* story of Santa Claus or how he'd begun his career as a North Pole fitness expert.

"And you people call me a Grinch. Fine, I'll tell you the story. Can't believe none of you know it."

Miranda was watching him, smiling.

"I know it," she said.

Douglas did a double-take. "You do?"

"Yeah, you're referring to the story of St. Nick's Gym?"

Douglas smiled back. Something else they had in common! Or maybe she was just getting bored of being an observer here. Either way, he felt his chest lighten.

"I sure am. Wanna help me tell it?"

Miranda checked around the room, waiting for approval or disapproval. Most of Douglas's coworkers were staring back, their faces growing more vacant by the second. When no one reacted, Miranda shrugged and nodded. "Sure."

"Okay then. So, St. Nick's Gym."

He adjusted his position to get more comfortable, leaned against the back of his chair, and folded his arms over his belly. The problem with the story of St. Nick and his gym was that it took a while to tell it, and Douglas didn't want to utter the first word without getting comfortable. He also needed a moment to remember how it started. It had been years since he'd last heard it, and his grandfather was a much better storyteller than he was.

He cleared his throat anyway. No time like the present to begin the storyteller theatrics.

"If anyone could bring us some water, that would be great," he said.

St. Nick's Gym

1.

WHEN HE WAS BUT a youth, the world had not yet heard the name of "St. Nicholas." No, not even a whisper nor a shout could be heard among the villagers, nor the townsfolk, nor the city dwellers across the land, claiming that a man such as he had lived or breathed, much less traveled the globe to work where they worked, or eat where they ate, or dance where they danced. Not so much as a rumor nor a fleeting thought had his name written upon it, built to infect conversation or shape the behavior of children. To the world around him, the name of St. Nicholas did not exist, nor did anyone believe it should exist. In those days, he was no more famous than you or I. To all but a select few, he was simply a nobody, a commoner, a snowflake to melt under the sun.

No, when he was but a young man, approximately two hundred years of age (or about twenty-five in mortal years), "Jolly" St. Nick, or Santa Claus as he is known today, was an unknown to children, to chimneys, and to the spirit of Christmas the world over. When the kiddies spoke of presents and holiday wishes, writing their requests in intelligible scribble on long scrolls of parchment, they submitted their wish lists to the unlikeliest of Christmas deliverymen, their parents. And in those days of old, when parents were poor, and a good year was a year that no one died, expecting a gift for Christmas was a long-shot, and receiving one was a miracle. Yes, the children would ask for presents anyway, and sometimes they even asked for something fun, like a toy, but, alas, the Christmas spirit was weak, for the children would wake up on that cold December morning with naught in their stockings but a lump of coal, and not for a lack of goodness, but rather for the good of the oven in which they needed fuel to keep warm.

No, the name of St. Nick was absent from the lips of all who would one day come to believe. His name was spoken only among those circles of elite who dwelled in the deep north, and only out of rumor, not of fact. Yes, he was still known by a select few. But he was not known as the figure of charity that he has become today. He was known simply for his niche specialties as a powerlifter of reindeer and a hobbyist toymaker, and, according to the world stage, these things were not yet that important, to the world, or in general.

In those early days, St. Nick did not have a toy workshop, per se, but he did own a gym that was slightly larger than the average northern bedroom. Because he was reclusive, he kept his gym private, and because the building was so small, he owned only one piece of equipment, a treadmill. But every month he would add another extension to the building that would increase its original size by 50%, and with each extension he would add a new piece of equipment—a weightlifting bench, a leg press, a dry canoe—so that he could build up not only his gym, but his body, too! Of course, he would work out night and day, day and night, buffing his biceps, toning his pecs, and sculpting his abs like a champion. He would lift reindeer from his weight bench, push his legs against an iceberg tip tilted ominously over a log, and simulate paddling in the canoe that never moved to increase his mass. He would tell himself at the height of his pain, "You can do it, Nick! Never give up!" And he would work out, night and day, day and night, until his body was dehydrated but undoubtedly looking good.

When summer came, and the ice softened, and the polar bears awoke from their long six-month naps, he would spend his days researching advances in biology, and then use the wooden resources he had around him to build fitness equipment that would maximize his muscle growth. He would hike a hundred miles in the snow toward Canada or Siberia until he found the choicest of conifers in which to chop into logs. Then he would hike a hundred miles back to his gym, dragging the logs behind, until he could dump them into his growing resource pile. Then he would hike a hundred miles to Canada or Siberia again to repeat the process until he had a stack of logs that stood as high as his roof. As winter neared, buff St. Nick would toss a handful of logs into the fire, turning them to coal, and then he would transfer the coal to the oven that he kept in the northwest corner of the gym, and fire any sand he collected along the way into glass. Then he would whittle the wood down to fine-cut planks, using the forward motion of his arms with extra wide strokes, leaning forward and back to maximize the strain on his muscles, until he had enough to build the frame for another invention in which he could use to build his body. It was in this way that he could craft his home, his equipment, and his livelihood, bettering himself, and his body, and his self-esteem, and it kept him healthy, and it kept him energized, and he would continue to better himself in this way for the next fifty years (or six years and two and a half months in normal mortal years).

Yes, St. Nick was happy to continue this routine. He didn't bother anyone, and no one bothered him. But deep down he wasn't satisfied. Even though he kept his spirits in check, he wasn't feeling jolly. Every day he'd spend on his workout equipment, he would grunt and sweat and yell at himself for not pushing himself harder, and he would punch his mirror whenever he'd look at himself because he just wasn't "there" yet. He ate a diet of roots and imported blueberries, and sometimes a reindeer if one had died of starvation. But his lean diet didn't make him feel good, and neither did the "burn" he felt in his muscles. Even when he took his summer hikes to Canada or Siberia and got some fresh air and sunshine, he felt empty inside. And he didn't know why. So, he continued to build more equipment, continued to push himself harder, and continued to spend many nights screaming in pain at the cramps he'd suffer after each intense workout. *I just need to push harder*, he often thought.

In those times when he couldn't push himself harder, he would retreat to a corner of his gym and whittle a figurine out of his leftover wood scraps. Most of his figurines were just versions of himself, but leaner, buffer, and more distinguished. The first time he built a figurine, he carved it whole from a single scrap of wood. Then he placed it on a shelf that he had also carved out of wood. Over the course of that first year, he would spend his time away from the workout, carving as many as a hundred figurines, each one more defined than the last. But, because St. Nick could not limit himself to the same old routine without risking a loss in shape—in this case, his creative shape—he spent his second year crafting figurines with moving parts, using interwoven pine needles as joints. In his third year, St. Nick decided to give his figurines color, so he hiked farther south that summer to gather flowers and berries, and then ground them into colored pastes on his return. He carved a small handle out of a scrap of wood and plucked the hairs out of his reindeers' tails to create a paintbrush. He would continue to improve his toy-making craft alongside his gym-making craft, making bigger and better figurines each year until they could no longer fit on the shelf. Within ten years, he found himself making life-sized mannequins and posting them outside the gym as bouncers, warning weary travelers to stay away. But he was still unsatisfied. He wondered if it was because his mannequins were naked, and his own clothes were falling apart. So, he tried cloth-making to go along with his toy-making and his gym-making.

In the summers when he'd travel south to find his choicest pinewood, flowers, and berries, he would also kidnap a few sheep and bring them back to his gym at the North Pole. He kept a sled on hand to help him transport his growing supply of goods and resources. Whenever the sheep died from the cold, he'd throw their remains onto the sled. This kept him from pulling his back out. Once he'd returned to the gym, he would shear the wool off their bodies and fashion it into cloth. Then he would stitch the cloth to other pieces to create a shirt, a jacket, or a pair of socks. St. Nick did not know of the fashions trending in the nations to his south, but he did know what he liked, and he liked the color red. So, he dyed the wool in cranberry juice and fashioned his first set of clothing for himself. Whatever he had leftover, he fashioned for his mannequins. And with his new stylish threads, he felt he had accomplished something wonderful. But he was still unsatisfied.

At this point, miserable St. Nick didn't know what to do with himself.

That's when he had a visitor come knocking on his door.

2.

After spending a long night running on the treadmill, St. Nick was startled to hear the knock on his gym door. He had thought his mannequins would deter such distractions, but he was clearly mistaken. When he answered the door, he saw a little man with pointy ears standing there with a cup nestled in his outstretched hand. The little man, who wore green pants and a frown, introduced himself as Buddy, an elf.

"Never heard of you," St. Nick told his visitor in the spaces between his heavy panting.

"I come from a village to the west," Buddy the elf said.

"I have nothing you want," St. Nick said. "Why come at all?"

The saddened elf could barely make eye contact with St. Nick when asked the question, but he did his best to answer anyway.

"We are an impoverished people and I—I've come looking for work."

St. Nick valued his privacy, and he did not like the idea of anyone coming around to bother him or to use his stuff, and he certainly did not like the idea of having to *pay* someone to hang around him all day. So, he told the young elf to get lost. Then he bolted his door shut to make sure the elf didn't try to sneak in somehow.

But the message was lost on the elf. He knocked again and again until grumpy St. Nick unlocked the door and opened it. When St. Nick asked him again what he wanted, the sad elf stuck to his story.

"My village is about to die," he said. "My people need employment if we are to feed ourselves."

St. Nick thought about Buddy's plight a little longer than before. He considered what it was like to live in poverty. But he decided that he, too, was impoverished, and the difference between him and the elf was that he took care of himself, and the elf clearly needed others to take care of him for him. St. Nick was a doer, not a waiter, so he decided not to wait to do what needed done.

"I feel for you," he said. "So, here's what I'm going to do. I'm going to say no. Not because I don't care, but because I do care. As you return to your village, you can think about how."

Buddy looked wounded, and St. Nick did not understand why. The greatest thing he could do for this elf, and for this elf's people, was to teach him about the ways of the world. Buddy needed to know that the world was restrictive, discriminating, and cruel. He needed to know the world was not a charitable place. The world was out only for itself. Surely Buddy would've—no, Buddy *should*'ve understood the gift wise St. Nick was giving him, the gift of knowledge. Or, if he didn't, he could figure it out as he returned to his village.

"Please, sir," the elf said. "We need a job, or we will starve."

"Then do as I do and eat roots and dead reindeer," said resourceful St. Nick.

"We cannot travel far, for the land is harsh. Those who have ventured far have never returned."

"Traveling takes practice. And muscle." St. Nick noticed how scrawny the young elf was. "You need to build your body, and your skill. When you've done both, then you can fend for yourself."

"How can I build my body without food? How can I build my skill without work?"

St. Nick thought about the elf's questions. Several times he attempted to answer them. Each time he stopped before he spoke, second-guessing the response he was about to give. He could see that Buddy had posed a more difficult situation for him to consider, one not so easily dismissed. It was true that the body needed food before it could grow stronger. It was true that skill could increase only when practiced often. And even though he could argue that traveling a little farther from the village each journey was a nice and steady way to progress in skill, one that could almost guarantee a return, St. Nick could not ignore the one core problem that Buddy had posed, the problem that the poor elf had no matter what he did on his own: no elf could build his body without food, and no elf could return from a long trip if he starved to death on his practice journey. Simply telling the elf to find a way and then shut the door in his face wouldn't have taught him anything. So, he thought about the conditions the elf must've lived in and thought about how the elf could grow in his strength and skill from where he lived. The answer came to him when he thought about how best to find food where none seemed to grow.

"You must dig through the ice," St. Nick said. "Dig until you find earth. And then build a fire to keep the ice from coming back. Then plant a tree and eat from it when it grows fruit. The digging will give you strength. The planting will give you character."

"It is barren here in the North Pole. No tree would ever survive. And we do not have the tools in which to dig."

St. Nick began to wonder how these people ever survived in the first place.

"We used to barter for our food," Buddy said. "But we can no longer pay the merchant who comes here in the summer. It is why we need a job."

St. Nick thought about it some more. Surely there was something they could do to take care of themselves without the need of him, or of their precious traveling merchant. The answer finally came to him, just as he was about to concede that there were no more answers.

"Survival of the fittest," he said. "You fight your brethren to the death and eat the losers. Strength, character, survival— everything you could ever want."

The elf was horrified by his last answer. The more he thought about it, the more he was horrified by it, too.

"Okay, bad plan, but I have nothing else," he said. "You have a troubling problem to be sure, one beyond even my knowledge."

The elf was mystified. His face trembled; then he grew hot with anger. The reclusive St. Nick felt something in his own chest that he had never felt before. There was some kind of tension taking over. The hairs on his skin rose. He felt something akin to . . . fear. He began to wonder if this desperate elf was sizing him up for character assassination. That was, perhaps, the last thing a person needed, especially one trying to better himself in every way. Suddenly, he felt compassion for the elf, as if it were a long-forgotten defense mechanism kicking in to save him.

"Maybe I'll see if I can find *something* for you to do around here," he said.

And so began the relationship between St. Nick and his elves.

3.

History may show a modification to the truth, as is the case when people stop believing in it, but no one who knew the whole truth could've expected St. Nick and the elves to get along like old chums, at least not right off the bat. Tensions surrounded them at every turn for months. But they made the effort to work together without conflict. Sometimes they had a good day. Sometimes not. They had what we might today call a "traditional working relationship."

When the elves arrived on their first day of work, they were overly joyed, and St. Nick was already feeling apprehension over his decision. Because he was a dour fella who wanted to be left alone to enjoy his workouts in peace, he could not get used to the idea of having dozens of little men and women buzzing about, asking him about his day, wondering what they could work on today. Many times, he had wanted to tell them to get lost, that this new plan was never going to work. But the elves were so diligent, so determined to bring home something of value for the traveling merchant, that they ignored his warnings about termination in favor of giving all their attention to the job at hand, which he had decided would involve helping him build a new piece of gym equipment. Even as they asked him questions about what his gym was for, how the existing equipment worked, and how he wanted them to build the next piece, he found it difficult to deny their tenacity. He found it almost uncanny how focused they were once they got their mind set on something, not too unlike himself.

Because he couldn't throw them right into the fire—figuratively or literally—he decided to spend the first few days training them on how to set the tools and prepare the materials for construction. They had assured him that they knew some fundamentals of construction—they had, after all, built their own village at some point long ago—but he wanted to hear nothing of that. St. Nick's attitude was that his job would be done his way, and he would have to help them unlearn their ways for them to learn his ways. So, he used the first day to break them down so he could build them up.

"You are nothing but maggots," he told them, after he had forced them to stand in a row out in the snow. "You'll never amount to anything. You are useless to me, and you are useless to yourselves."

The elves began to cry.

"Do not cry, you maggots! You get tough!"

They cried with more gusto.

"Quit yer cryin' and tell me 'yes, sir'!"

They didn't quit their crying, but they did tell him, "Yes, sir!"

Demanding St. Nick quickly saw the work he had cut out for him, so he put the name-calling on hold until he could establish some trust. They didn't know him, and he didn't know them, so outright comparing them to slimy critters that ate garbage and dead flesh was probably not the best way to begin a relationship, he realized. Even though he had no experience talking to people, especially to a group of elves, he wasn't certain that was the case. But it seemed right.

Instead, he herded them into the gym and showed them how the equipment worked.

"First you get on the belt," he said, when he stepped on the treadmill. They had gathered in the corner and marveled as they watched him climb aboard. Their eyes were wide, their mouths open, and they made sounds of wonder that convinced him he was quickly becoming a cult leader. "Then you press the button."

He ran on the treadmill for about thirty minutes, and the elves continued to watch him awestruck. When he stopped the machine, he asked if any of them wanted to give it a try. Every hand in the room went up.

"Okay, so here's how it works. Each of you is very small. Because your legs are so short, it's possible the speed settings will inadvertently suck you under the belt. You probably won't want that, so I'd advise you buddy up and run on the slowest speed. That way, if one of you can't keep up, the other can push you off before you go under. Sound good?"

"Yes, sir!"

St. Nick was glad to hear them answering back in the tough way he had instructed them, but he didn't want to show it. Part of building toughness was to withhold any affection or sense of value. That's what seemed right.

"Good, now get on the machine, two at a time. I'll set the speed for you since you probably can't reach the panel. You've got fifteen minutes to get used to it. Go!"

The injuries that day were fewer than he had anticipated.

Once everyone had gotten a sense of how the machines worked, he moved them to the tool bench.

"This is a screwdriver," he said, when he showed them the first tool. "You use this to tighten small metal rods into holes or bolts to fasten two larger pieces together. The small metal rod, which you can see has these coiled grooves running up its entire surface, is called a screw. The screw is an essential component for keeping pieces held together. Any questions?"

One of the elves in the corner raised her hand. St. Nick pointed at her.

"Yes?"

"We already know what these tools are," she said. "We have them ourselves. We've built our village ourselves. We built it using tools just like these."

St. Nick growled and threw the screwdriver at the elf. It narrowly missed her head as she ducked.

"You will learn things my way," said the irritated St. Nick.

It took him several days to teach the elves about the tools and how each one worked, and it took several more to show them how to handle the materials necessary for building the gym equipment, which included wooden planks, some pine needles, rare metals, and a gummy substance that he referred to as "rubber." At every step the elves tried to convince him that they already knew how the basic materials worked and how to shape them into more effective materials, but he wanted them to learn things his way, so he continued to throw sharp objects at them until they understood.

The injuries those days were fewer than he had anticipated.

When it came time to finally begin building the new gym equipment, a celebration rang out among the elves. They were excited because they could now work, and this was the moment when their hours would start converting into payment. Even before St. Nick rang the bell, they had their tools in hand and determination on their faces. Once the bell rang, St. Nick had to jump out of the way, for they swarmed into the gym like rodents converging onto a piece of cheese.

St. Nick still wanted his privacy once the elves began, but he was softening about having them around. However, the second week of elvish employment changed his tune. The elves, who were much better builders than he had anticipated, had somehow snuck their entire village through the barren wasteland and built it up around his workshop overnight, and their village was, in a word, huge. Next thing St. Nick knew, he had hundreds of elves bustling about within a short walk from his house, and he was no longer content with this arrangement.

"Okay, that's it!" he yelled. "Everyone out! Job's finished! Get out of here and don't come back!"

But the elves didn't move. They just laughed at him.

He realized sometime later that he had emboldened them to hold their ground. Now that they were hundreds strong, he was vastly outnumbered and overwhelmed. Technically, the elves now owned him, and the last thing he needed was an uprising against him. So, he let them stay.

4.

Of the many things that antisocial St. Nick had never had before now, the greatest he'd missed was friends. He'd spent as long as he could remember living in isolation, home empty and ice fields barren as far as the eye could see. Even though he'd felt an ache in his chest, he'd always attributed it to elements unseen. He never realized it had to do with living alone.

Years had gone by in that bubble called loneliness, yet he never knew that loneliness was the thing building a wall around his heart. Thanks to those annoying little elves buzzing about his workshop, he finally realized that having others around was necessary to end that aching feeling.

Or their presence, at least, helped to numb it.

For several years, he put up with the uncanny diligence of the elven population, which, thanks to his employ, was growing faster and stronger by the year, and his attitude toward them had gradually softened. But the ache of loneliness maintained its shadow over his heart, and he didn't know how to fix it. He observed the elves daily, attempting to crack the code to their happiness, but nothing made sense. They were all part of the same community, responsible for the same tasks, yet they reveled in happiness more than he did. *Were they delusional? Had they purchased some kind of herb from the traveling merchant that inspired happiness?*

The truth was that confused St. Nick did not understand the inner workings of an elf, nor did he understand how doing the same job, the same way, day after day, year after year, kept them so jovial. They had food now, whereas they were starving when he'd first met them. And he had given them work, whereas before they had nothing to give them purpose. But the weather was still bitter, and they didn't have coats to protect them from the cold, and they were still very, very low to the ground. He had more possessions than they had, but they had more joy. And he could not figure out why they were so happy. And not knowing what made them happy just angered him even more.

Then, one summer, when St. Nick was traveling to Canada to gather his yearly stock of wood and sheep, he came to discover a mysterious something that might've answered his teasing question. And, as he discovered this new ripple in his usual understanding, he finally figured out what that one thing was that the elves had that he never had for himself.

And he discovered it purely by chance.

He had planned on visiting his usual spot in the Saskatchewan area, as he was used to it and knew of everything it could offer, but this year, adventurous St. Nick decided to try something different. He headed deeper south and east into the mysterious regions of Nova Scotia to find his plunder. It was there, somewhere near its Atlantic shore, that he finally found the answer to his nagging question.

It was there that he met Martha W. Valentine, the future Mrs. St. Nick.

Martha was immediately taken by the buff lumberjack invading her backyard, both figuratively and literally, as he was searching for the best trees about fifty feet from her window near the edge of her property: the sight of his rippling biceps and quivering abs made her weak inside, but the sight of her supple cheeks and her dark porcelain doll hair caused a similar reaction in him when he saw her staring back, so he broke in and stole her from her bedroom before she had a chance to protest, which she didn't bother with because he was every Greek statue she'd ever seen in the flesh, and she wanted to wake up to the sight of that every morning. He just realized she had parts different than his, and it excited him, so he didn't care if she was beautiful or not—he didn't really know if she was beautiful, for he never got far enough in his feminine research to figure out what the rest of the world considered beautiful, or what a guy of his proportions should've been naturally attracted to. It was all much too complicated for him, so he didn't give it much thought once he'd brought her back to the workshop and made her his wife.

Anyway, St. Nick became jolly that night and his unidentified ache went away.

5.

A few days after his marriage to Martha began, jolly St. Nick began expressing himself through a catchphrase.

"Ho ho ho," he'd often say every morning, to express the newfound joy in his heart.

Eventually the elves caught onto his catchphrase, and they, too, began to use it.

"Ho ho ho," they'd respond in kind.

Because it was his thing, St. Nick eventually had to whip them. But he let them enjoy themselves for a while. It was a fun thing to say.

But, as time progressed, and the thrill of having a partner in his life began to equalize with the rest of his daily routine, his old attitudes began to resurface, and the next thing he knew, he was back to business, treating the elves like employees rather than as friends, and his life found a new balance that kept him content for the next ten years, but not necessarily happy.

One day when he was buffing the side of his rowing machine, an elf came to him crying. He didn't ask what was wrong or offer any compassion that might calm the elf down. He simply stared at him. When the elf saw that he would do nothing more to acknowledge his grief than to fix his gaze upon him, he broke down into a smattering mess of explaining things.

"I'm sorry, I'm sorry, I'm sorry," the elf said. "I didn't mean to do it. I tried to stop it, but I couldn't. It just happened. I'm sorry I'm sorry I'm sorry."

St. Nick said nothing. He just stared.

"It won't happen again. Promise. I'm so sorry."

St. Nick went back to buffing the side of his rowing machine.

"I didn't mean to break the treadmill," the elf said. "I thought I could train our reindeer to run faster. Didn't mean to ruin the belt. So sorry, so sorry, please don't kill me."

St. Nick wiped a layer of grime off the rowing machine and tossed the rag to his side. Then he grabbed another rag and wiped off another layer.

"Please forgive me. I'm so sorry."

St. Nick tossed the new rag on top of the old one. Then he stared at the elf. The elf's eyes were wide in their plea for mercy.

"So sorry."

Finally, St. Nick shrugged, then went back to polishing the rowing machine.

The elf walked away confused, clearly thinking he was about to receive the beating of a lifetime. But St. Nick didn't have the heart for it. Truth was, he was beginning to tire of his job, and he didn't care anymore if something broke around here.

When he went to bed that night, he told Martha what had happened. In her usual calming way, she told him what was wrong.

"You're stuck in a rut. Change it up a little, eh?"

He scoffed at her.

"What are you talking about? I don't get stuck in ruts."

"Everyone gets stuck in a rut eventually. It's called repetition and boredom. You make gym equipment all the time. Make something else. It'll make you feel better, eh?"

When he told her he was at a loss for ideas, she reminded him that he used to make dolls and mannequins for fun.

"I have too many bodies standing around here already," he told her. "It's not really the change I need."

She winked at him.

"Try it anyway. It's different. You used to enjoy it, right?"

He shrugged.

"I guess so."

"Good, problem solved. Now let me sleep."

The next day, he took his wife's advice. And she was right; he did feel better making something different. In fact, it energized him. So, he kept making toys. And the momentum took over faster than he thought possible. When the elves caught on to his new plan, dolls came cranking out into existence by the minute.

St. Nick's workshop had suddenly come close to bursting from having so many toys cluttering the floor. There were so many dolls lying around that they began spilling into his living quarters. And, even though he was pleased with his newfound creative energy, Martha was not as pleased, and she had given him an ultimatum.

"I know you needed a change," she told him. "But this is ridiculous. Either the toys go, or I go."

St. Nick was proud of his inventions, and he was proud of the collection he had built up over those few productive months, so her ultimatum had left him slightly heartbroken, and confused. But he hadn't made the kind of toy that could keep him jolly, so he acquiesced to his wife's request and threw the pile of dolls into the snow.

And for days he'd stare at the pile as it grew taller and taller, wishing he had someplace better to store those toys. But for the life of him he couldn't think of an ideal location, for the village was already filled with his newest inventions, and even the elves were tired of looking for places to put them.

It was then that Martha provided him with an idea.

"Why don't you just get rid of them?" she asked. "What purpose do they serve you?"

St. Nick had spent his life hoarding his inventions, and he wasn't ready to throw them out.

"Because I don't want to."

What he didn't tell her was that he didn't know how to. But he knew in his heart that Martha was right. He didn't need any of this stuff. It was rare that he ever looked at these toys again. In fact, even his gym equipment he'd hardly used anymore. It was the thrill of building something new that had formed his attachment to them. They didn't make his life better. They just got in the way.

But how could he get rid of them? That was the question he didn't know how to answer.

"I really don't know what to do anymore," he said.

She gave him a hard look.

"Your first problem is that you build things for yourself," Martha said, "and you're overstuffed. You need to make a change."

St. Nick argued that making a change was her last suggestion, and the reason he had so much junk stacking up outside in the first place. Making a change was the last thing he needed to do.

She simply put her hand on his cheek and smiled.

"You're thinking too selfishly. That's always been your problem. Think about others for a change. You won't find contentment until you do."

St. Nick stared at her as if she were resting her head under a piston. Thinking of others was not his forte. But then he remembered how he'd felt after the elves first came to work for him, and how he'd felt when he'd brought Martha home for the first time, and it occurred to him that the aches in his heart had always found comfort whenever he'd allow someone new into his life. So, he voiced the thought in his head for a second opinion.

"Should I kidnap a new bride?" he asked her. "Is that the change I need?"

Martha lost her smile, and he didn't know why. Then she slapped him across the face. He still didn't know why.

"No, that is not the change you need. Think more charitably, eh?"

"I should invite a new bride to kidnap me?"

Martha slapped him again. She had a lot of power in the flat of her hand, probably due to the workouts she'd been doing for the last ten years.

"Make gifts for people," she finally said. "Instead of hoarding them, make dolls for children. Make tools for adults. Make treadmills for the unhealthy. Don't make them for yourself."

St. Nick had trouble looking at her after that. He couldn't believe she was suggesting that he gave his hard work away for free. That was crazy talk. Who was this woman he had married?

"The pain you feel in your heart comes from being selfish," she said. "Bless the children with toys if you really want it all to go away. That's how you get rid of that mountain outside. That's how you make yourself happy. That's how you make *me* happy."

Skeptical St. Nick didn't care much for his wife's advice, but she had yet to steer him wrong, so he decided to give her suggestion a chance. So, when the summer came and the ice began to soften, he threw all his spare toys on a sled and dragged them through the wilderness down into Canada or Siberia and passed them out to any child he could find playing in the streets. Even though their parents tried to attack him out of fear that he was up to no good, the children walked away with a smile. They now had something they were never given the privilege of having before. They now had a toy to play with.

St. Nick didn't feel any kind of emotional change when he returned to the North Pole, so he ordered his elves to build him another series of dolls. He thought maybe the sensation of joyful giving hadn't found its way through his skin yet, and he wanted to give it another try. So, with his second set, he traveled south again, this time in the opposite direction. Even though the results were similar with the children he found in the newer location, the feeling he had in his heart was different. Now he was noticing the difference. Now he was beginning to under-stand the value of his new line of work. Children who grew up with nothing but a frown on their faces could now go home with a smile, something which he'd never had himself before meeting Martha. Now it finally made sense.

He went out a few more times throughout that year, making sure to hit different parts of Canada and Siberia, where he could find desperate children and drop off his new line of mannequin loot. He also experimented with giving the children clothes to wear, but he found they were less as thrilled about receiving socks as they were about receiving toys, so he stuck to his mandate of making only things kids would want to play with.

By the end of the year, he had stockpiled his greatest cache of dolls and mannequins, while tossing in a few experimental baubles like toy animals and fake tools (for those who wanted to be like their parents), and on one embarrassing moment, tossing in an elf, which he had to apologize for later, but never got around to it since apologies weren't really his thing, and dragged his sled the farthest south he had ever gone in a toy drive: Moscow.

It was there that his name began to go viral.

For the next two years, he would revisit the same places, giving the same kinds of toys, and each time the children would cry out to their parents, "Saint Nick is here! Saint Nick is here!" The parents were still uneasy about having this muscular man in a red suit giving their children playthings, especially on an annual basis, but they gradually accepted his charity when he began giving them exercise equipment and power tools to play with.

But with word of his name spreading like wildfire, and regions where he'd never set foot starting to also chant his name, the news had come back to him that the rest of the world was eager for its dose of St. Nick's generosity. By the time his name had circulated throughout the nations and each nationality had done its job in butchering it, he discovered that the world had no longer known him as St. Nick, but as Santa Claus. He had no idea how such miscommunication could garble up something so simple as his name, but he decided he liked the change—something about it was catchy, almost brand-like. So, he ran with it.

Yes, the demand for his charity grew hot overnight. But he soon realized how economically destructive handling everyone's request would've been under his current system of order fulfillment and delivery, so he had a brainstorm session with Buddy, his elf commander-in-chief, about how to keep up with the influx of requests.

After many agonizing nights of budgeting resources and designing the quickest production schedule they could afford, St. Nick went to work scouring the entire Arctic Circle for hidden elvish villages, immediately hired any elf he could find within range, and gave them permission to rebuild their homes in and around his workshop. Within a few days, he had multiplied his current elven population by five, and his village of elves had turned into a city of elves.

He also had to refurbish his workshop to handle not only the new demand, but the new storage space required to hold the massive boost in inventory he and his elves were about to create. So, he and the elves went to work on expanding his workshop, not only outward, but upward, too. They built several new wings on either side of the original gym, and a complete factory floor over the dead center of the North Pole. Building the factory right over the pole allowed for more balanced testing of things like compasses and magnets, so he was happy about the move. He also ordered several new floors added to the workshop so that each fleet of elves could work on a different product line from the ones working on the floor below. That meant keeping a steady influx of variety, and a greater range of happiness for each diverse child in the world. Soon, he could build not only dress-up dolls for the girls, but action dolls for the boys, as well as snow globes, mechanical creatures, and anything else his elves' imaginations could develop.

The final logistical problem he had was with delivery. Simply leaving the village every month to make a toy run down south was not helping his production speed, and dragging it hundreds of miles through the snow by his own two feet was also too slow. So, he and his elves worked out a plan to involve the reindeer. He figured he could tie a couple of them to the sled and force them to drag him across the wasteland at a much faster speed than he could walk himself. When they brainstormed the perfect number, they decided four would be enough. The sled, after all, was not that large. But even as they prepped it for delivery, they encountered another problem. Because St. Nick had decided he would make only one trip a year, at the beginning of winter when the rest of the world was experiencing the same cold he had felt year-round, he discovered that a year's worth of toys created quite the mountain of crap, and stacking it all on that tiny little sled was almost impossible. And, even if he could've wedged it all together, four reindeer would not have had the power required to drag it and still maintain optimal speed. So, he and his elves built an emergency sleigh capable of holding as much as eight times the sled's limit, decided to up the reindeer limit to eight, well, nine on those nights that he needed to use the red-nosed one to see in the dark, and then raced out across the tundra to deliver those gifts before the New Year had a chance to throw him off schedule.

The reconstruction effort paid off. He was able to visit far more villages in far more regions than he had previously been able to reach on his own. And now the kids were screaming his name, "Santa!" as if he were a popular concert pianist.

But he still had one logistical problem that he could not overcome no matter what new modifications he had given his sleigh. He couldn't travel across oceans or reach islands in the middle of nowhere. His sleigh wasn't equipped to float, and his reindeer, unfortunately, couldn't swim. So, he asked his wife, Martha, for some help.

"Here, let me have a look," she said.

She came back to him a short while later with a solution.

"Just say, 'On Dancer, on Prancer,' and list all of their names in a row when you need to get somewhere impossible to reach in a hurry."

The following year, when St. Nick went out to make his annual delivery, he took his wife's advice, and without breaking even the slightest sweat, he was able to travel in one night with his reindeer as far south as Brazil, where it was still summer. Because Martha was from Canada, she was able to teach the reindeer how to fly.

6.

As St. Nick's popularity blew up the following years, the children of the world decided it was time to give a little something back to him. They were certainly grateful for all the gifts that he'd brought them each year, but they were beginning to lose satisfaction. One-way giving didn't carry the appeal for them that it had in the beginning. They didn't know how to give back, of course—if any of them knew how to make toys, then they wouldn't have needed him in the first place. But then the world changed. Just as St. Nick needed a spark to begin the cycle of charitable giving, so, too, did the children, and their giving began with one child setting the precedent.

St. Nick hadn't quite gotten used to air travel, even after five years, so he was prone to dizziness and air sickness. On the night of his fifth annual gift delivery, he had lost track of where he was, so he could've been anywhere. But he kept to his plan, and dropped in on any house that he could find with a stuffed animal lying in the yard, the signal that a child lived there. That night, the night that the world had changed, had been full of the standard routine—swoop down, say hello to the children who were standing outside waiting for him, then toss them whatever gift from the bag they wanted, then fly off to the next house.

But one household dared to be different than the rest that evening. The child who lived there waited for him, as was the tradition for the time, but he wasn't alone. He had with him a plate stacked with cookies and a glass full of milk. When St. Nick tossed the child a small box that released a clown after turning a crank a few clicks, the child tossed him the cookies and milk. St. Nick was reluctant to try this unusual food at first. But the child, in his eagerness to make his gift-giving hero happy, stared at him with wide eyes and an expectant face, and St. Nick, who had come to realize that he liked the children of the world, did not want to disappoint the one standing before him, so he ate the cookies and drank the milk. And it was the greatest thing he had ever eaten, ever.

"You've done good, kid," he told the boy with a smile. "Real good."

And the boy, thrilled that St. Nick not only knew his name but liked his gift, ran into the house screaming to his parents that he had just gotten approval from Santa Claus.

The following year, St. Nick discovered that word about this exchange of gifts had gotten around, and now most of the children he visited had milk and cookies waiting for him. Because he couldn't refuse those innocent faces, he took and ate every cookie he was offered and drank every glass of milk he needed to wash it all down.

The next day he was very sick, but he decided it was worth it for the children. And he couldn't deny his newfound love for milk and cookies.

Then came the shocker. He realized he was moving a lot slower than usual.

The entire next year, he sat at his bench, building toy dolls for the following start of winter and the subsequent delivery, and forgot that he had a gym. When it came time to make the next delivery, word had spread across the globe that Santa Claus ate milk and cookies, and every home he visited had a plate waiting for him. By the time his deliveries ended for the year, he would come home sick to his stomach.

But that wasn't the worst of it.

The problem St. Nick faced now was a problem with image. Despite his early obsession with gym equipment, he had somehow gotten very, very fat.

When he saw himself in the mirror for the first time in years, surprised St. Nick couldn't believe his eyes. His godlike body had been blown out of proportion to such extremes that he had thought he was looking at himself through a trick mirror. Except, he wasn't. He looked down at his feet to discover that he could no longer see them.

He fell into a depression by January.

Martha tried to cheer him up, but he wouldn't listen to her. She kept trying to tell him that she still loved him, but he didn't believe her. He said he'd have to grow a beard now just to hide his fat face. He fell into a stupor. He spent many nights sleeping when he should've been working. Even when he tried getting onto the treadmill to reverse the negative effects of eating a ton of milk and cookies in one night, he found it very difficult to run. Part of it was due to him never repairing it after one of the reindeer had broken it. But even if it had worked, he couldn't move faster than a jog. The sudden pull of belly fat jiggling up and down felt like his stomach was trying to rip his chest off his body. It was very uncomfortable.

He was ashamed of himself. And he didn't want to be seen this way. He went into hiding for the rest of the year.

When December rolled back around, and it was once again time to prepare for delivery, St. Nick refused to come out of his room.

"I'm disgusting," he told Martha when she tried to lure him out.

"It's all in your head," she told him.

"No, look at me. I'm a tub. And please don't look at me. I'm a tub."

"But, honey! What of the children?"

"What of them?"

"If you don't deliver your gifts, their hearts will be broken."

"*My* heart is broken."

Martha had done all she could to urge him on, to get him into that sleigh, to deliver those gifts to those sweet little children. But he ignored her. He was going to spend the rest of his days hiding from the world. He couldn't let anyone see him this way.

She had grown frustrated with his reluctance and did all she could to get him out of bed and moving again. But all she could say to him was, "Remember the children."

St. Nick did remember the children. They were the ones who had driven him to this awful state of obesity, the little jerks.

He was determined to give up the charity. The people he had tried to help had turned around and ruined him. He thought they were horrible little trolls for making him so miserable. Then he thought the elves were horrible little trolls for encouraging their bad behavior in the first place. They were the reason he was able to get so many toys out to the world. Then he resented Martha for planting the seed of charity in his mind. She was the real reason he had gotten so fat. If she had just kept her mouth shut, he'd still look like Adonis.

As December marched on, Martha enacted a move of desperation to get her husband back to work. It was really the only move she had, and it was a longshot. But she went for it. St. Nick had spent the year falling into despair, and she had to get him out.

"This is who you are now," she said. "Yes, you were once a thing of beauty. But you were also miserable night and day. You threatened your elves' lives on many occasions. You ignored me for the sake of your own body. You lived a life of isolation to preserve your youth, and none of it made you happy. None of it made you who you are today. The children, they made you who you are today. The gifts you give them, they made you who you are today. And though you may not be happy with your body now, the children, I can tell you, do not care how you look. They care that you show up and bring them happiness. So, get out of bed and show them happiness before I divorce you and marry a young Austrian bodybuilder, eh?"

It took a little time for it to sink into St. Nick's mind, but he understood his wife's point. His life had changed from isolated misery to one of family and happiness, and his body was now fat with it. His overstuffed belly was a reminder that he was no longer grumpy St. Nick, but jolly St. Nick, and *jolly* and *belly* sounded a lot alike. But more importantly, he had become Santa Claus, the children's winter hero, and Santa Claus was a fatso, dangit!

So, Santa Claus got into his sleigh that year, determined to find his happiness again, determined to make the most of his new girth made by cookies and milk. And he set off to continue his now lifelong tradition. And he made sure that he didn't change a thing. Well, one thing: he hired a doctor to keep a tab on him. He didn't want to die of a heart attack in the middle of a delivery, after all.

Actually, two things: he wanted to start sneaking into houses via the chimney in the dead of night so that no one would have to see him, and so he wouldn't have to feel guilty telling the children to screw off the next time they tried to ram milk and cookies down his throat.

Of course, they figured out his new plan and left milk and cookies on the mantelpiece instead. He decided he'd just have to get used to being fat. He'd pay them back by keeping a naughty and nice list and a helping of coal for those who missed the latter. Kids hated playing with coal.

Chapter 8

WHEN DOUGLAS AND MIRANDA finished telling the story, Douglas scanned the room, nodding at anyone who was still listening. Most of the staff had left after the part where Santa threatened to starve the elves, but he'd pressed on, knowing that those still listening by the end would understand where he was coming from. By the time he delivered his happily ever after, however, only Miranda, Angela, and Winston were left. And Terrance. He'd finally come swiveling in from the hallway as Douglas got to the part about Santa and Mrs. Claus getting together, and plopped onto the nearest vacant chair, sliding down so low that the base of his cranium touched the plastic back edge. He was so tired and sweaty from walking back from the restaurant that he wasn't interested in Douglas's ribald tale of forbidden love. In fact, when the story ended, he had the strength only to ask where his present was.

"Douglas gave it to the woman there," Angela said.

Terrance shook his head, climbed off his chair, and swiped the stapler from Miranda's hand.

"You ain't taking my energy *and* my gift," he said. He lumbered out of the party room without looking back.

Angela said nothing when Terrance disappeared down the hall. She was too busy trying to stay upright on the pool table to add any more thoughts to the conversation.

"You understand I'm never gonna get that back from him, right?" Winston said.

Douglas nodded.

"I said I'd make it up to you."

"You could start by opening his card," Angela said. She corrected her posture. Once again, she was upright and ready to boss people around.

Douglas stuck his index finger along the corner of the envelope and jacked the lid open. No surprise inside. It was a card, with pictures of candy canes all over it. Just as he'd assumed. But after telling a long story that none of his coworkers were interested in hearing, he figured he'd owed it to Winston for sticking with him to the end. If nothing else, it would shut Angela up.

He slid the card out and read its face. There were no words. No messages. Just candy canes.

"Thanks," Douglas said. "Very festive."

"Open it, jackass," Angela said.

Douglas sneered at her. Not only was her holiday cheer wearing thin, but so was her charm. January Angela was making too early of an appearance.

Winston, meanwhile, held out his palms.

"It's okay," he said. "Douglas can open it when he's ready."

Angela nodded.

"True. Or he could open it now since it's in his hand."

Winston tilted his head.

"Fair enough. You'll have to forgive her," Winston said. "Angela helped me pay for it, so it's understandable she's insistent."

Angela glared at him.

"You're not supposed to say that. That's a secret."

Douglas bounced his attention between them. How dire were Winston's financial straits if Angela had to help him pay for a Christmas card?

After robbing him of his stapler, he had no choice but to give him the satisfaction of opening the card he'd bought for him.

So, he did.

Sixteen NBA tickets fell out.

For home games to Douglas's favorite team.

He nodded at himself.

He was a douche.

"I don't know what to say," Douglas said.

Angela jumped off the table and darted her finger at him.

"Say 'bah humbug,'" she said. "I dare you."

Douglas had no words. He stared at Angela and right through her at the same time. The smile on her face was beyond friendly. It was snide.

His eyes drifted toward Miranda. Hers was the only face he could look at right now. No judgment in her eyes. No guilt in his when he looked upon her. Yet, he should've felt guilty. He'd made a fool of himself in front of her on more than one occasion. But she was still there. And her face was warm.

"Hey, Winston," Douglas said, still looking at Miranda, "you wanna go with me to the first game?"

"I'd like that," Winston said.

"Me too."

Douglas smiled at Miranda.

"Great," Angela said. "Now if you'll excuse me, I need to find out why Niles never came back with the champagne. Don't forget you're staying late."

Douglas nodded. Gordon was the one who took Miranda's pitch seriously, not Angela, so he had no intention of staying late tonight.

Winston and Angela left him alone in the room with Miranda. Once their footfalls were clear of the hallway, Douglas started gathering up the tissue paper he'd used for wrapping.

"Sorry you couldn't keep your gift," he said.

Miranda shrugged. "Something tells me it was never meant for me."

Douglas smirked. That was obvious from the start.

"Not exactly the gift that the guy from *Die Hard* would've given the blonde girl."

"We don't know that."

"Suspicion."

"Probably." Miranda held his gaze for a moment. "But that depends on how well he knows her. My guess is that he knows her well. But the movie never explores it. They could've just met at the airport for all we know."

"Unlikely."

"But possible."

Douglas set the tissue paper in a pile on the table.

"If I'd been any smoother today, you think that could've been us?"

Miranda shrugged.

"Possibly."

Douglas nodded. He figured as much.

"Any chance that could still be us?"

He held her gaze as he awaited her response. But she said nothing. Instead, she reached for the pile of tissue paper and peeled a sheet free. Then she searched through her bag and produced a pen. She used it to scribble something on the paper. Whatever it was, it was short.

She handed him the scrap. He read it.

Merry Christmas

Douglas folded the paper in his hand and stuffed it in his pocket.

"No matter what happens," he said, "I'll treasure this gift."

He meant it.

"I've got one more for you," Miranda said.

She reached for another sheet of tissue paper. Wrote something else. Handed it to him.

"Merry Christmas," she said.

Douglas read the note.

It was Miranda's phone number.

"May I walk you to your car?" Douglas asked.

Miranda nodded. "You may."

As they left the room and wove through a sea of vomit in the hallway and through the main floor, Douglas studied the phone number in case he lost the paper.

"They gonna be all right?" Miranda asked.

"Huh?"

She pointed at the puddles of sick on the office floor.

"Oh, yeah. Probably. Same thing happened last year. It's one reason I usually leave the party early."

Miranda said nothing.

When they got to Miranda's car, she reached into the passenger seat and produced a wrapped box. It was a little longer than a brick. She handed it to him.

"What's this?" he asked.

"Since we're giving away things that belong to other people, I figured I'd do my part." She winked. "Enjoy."

"What is it?"

She shrugged.

"Don't know. Client gave it to me."

Douglas held it to his chest.

"I'll treasure it forever."

She touched his shoulder.

"You're a good storyteller, Douglas. I hope we can do it again sometime."

Douglas winked back. He had her number now. Plenty of time to tell her new stories.

"By the way," she said, as she headed for the driver side door, "rich people drink wine at restaurants, not soft drinks. And truth serum is injected into your bloodstream, not your drink. Thought you'd like to know."

"Huh?"

"The story you told at lunch. I know you're taking creative license, but a little realism helps to sell it better."

His chest lightened. Sounded like she'd forgiven him for that.

"I wasn't prepared to think it through," he said. "A bit out of practice."

She winked at him. "But practice makes perfect."

"I'll do my best."

After Miranda left, Douglas returned to the office to gather his things. But before he left himself, he stopped by Gordon's office and peeked inside. Gordon was busy typing something on his computer. A plate of cookies sat on his desk untouched.

"Heading out," Douglas told him. "Merry Christmas."

Gordon looked up and smiled.

"Merry Christmas to you."

"Thanks for your help earlier. I got her number."

"Any time." He glanced at the box in Douglas's hand. "That your gift from the exchange?"

Douglas looked at it. "No, Miranda gave it to me."

"How nice. You should open it."

Douglas shrugged. Normally, he'd want privacy, but since it was a random gift not meant for him, he didn't see the harm. So, he pulled the paper away to find a wooden box. Inside was a vape pen.

"You a smoker?" Gordon asked.

"No."

"So, what are you going to do with it?"

Douglas didn't know. But he didn't want a nice gift from Miranda to go to waste.

"I'll think of something," he said.

"Sounds good. Okay, I have to get back to work. Dad wants the annual report in time for Christmas, and I'm still in February."

Douglas nodded.

"Okay." He headed for the door but stopped before he reached the handle. "Oh, just to let you know, half the staff vomited on the main floor again."

Gordon shook his head.

"Thanks for the head's up."

He shoveled the plate of cookies into the trash.

"Merry Christmas, Gordon."

"Merry Christmas, Douglas."

Douglas opened the office door. It was time to head home for the holidays.

(The Story Continues in Part 2: "Happy New Life")

HAPPY
NEW
LIFE

Chapter 1

JUST AFTER FIVE O'CLOCK on a Monday night, Douglas McCray dashed past Sally the receptionist without a good-bye or a "Happy New Year" and raced for his car. Sally might've been offended by his lack of response after she uttered a word out of her mouth Douglas couldn't comprehend, but he had no time to care. He had a hot date in two hours, and he didn't want to be late.

Miranda had entered his life exactly one week ago when she tried convincing his company's managers to buy a printing package for books and brochures that would inform visitors about operations here at Riche Fertilizer Solutions, but she exited almost as quickly. After giving him a secondhand gift of a vape pen after he'd given her a secondhand gift of a stapler—which she couldn't keep thanks to the original recipient showing up at the last minute to claim it for himself, the greedy bastard—Miranda got in her car and drove off into the sunset.

But not before giving Douglas her phone number.

It was a classic game of cat and mouse, where Miranda played the part of the mouse, and Douglas played the part of the guy who had to call the mouse if he ever wanted to see her again, which he very much wanted. In fact, after spending all of three hours that night telling himself to stay cool, he ditched his cool cat role and picked up the phone to call her. He even got as far as dialing nine out of ten numbers before telling himself to get a hold of himself and hang up.

And Douglas was about to hang up. He hovered his thumb over the button to disconnect. But he slipped and pressed the last number of Miranda's phone number instead. And not to outdo his mistake, his thumb slipped *again* and landed on the green call button.

Well, it was too late for him to hang up now, so he stayed on the line and waited for either Miranda or her voicemail to pick up.

Her voicemail picked up.

So, again, he still had time to play it cool. He could've hung up without a word and saved himself the stigma of being that guy who couldn't control his impulse to call the woman he had the hots for. It would've been the cool thing to do. And he had the entire autoresponder message to talk himself into hitting that disconnect button.

Beep.

"Hi, Miranda, it's me Douglas McCray." Too late again. "We met at my fertilizer company today. We had lunch at Olive Farm. Talked about *Die Hard.* And I helped you make your sale, I think. Hopefully you made your sale. Sorry if you didn't. So, yeah, just saying hi."

Douglas shook his head. He had no idea what he was saying. But he'd risked so much to get her attention, and now that he'd also gotten her number, he didn't want to waste it.

"Actually, no, I wanted to call you because I liked spending time with you, and I was hoping we could do it again. Maybe not tonight, though that would be nice. But soon? Call me back. This is my number." He was about to hang up, but he stopped himself. "Merry Christmas if I don't hear back from you before tomorrow."

He didn't hear from her for three days. But when she finally called him back, she agreed to meet him for dinner on Saturday night.

Douglas was ecstatic. On Friday night, he went out to buy a new tie for the special occasion. He also picked up a new dinner jacket to go with it. If he was going to have dinner with Miranda on Saturday night, then he would make it count.

Then Saturday afternoon came, and Douglas had just finished putting on his deodorant when Miranda called.

"Hey, I hate to do this to you," she said, "but I have to cancel our dinner tonight. So sorry. Personal emergency."

Douglas's stomach lurched. He fumbled his bottle of deodorant.

"How come?"

"I just said. Personal emergency."

"Everything all right?"

"Not at the moment. I have to go. We'll try again next week."

Douglas's mind shut down. He blurted out the only thing his feeble thoughts could muster. Whether it was sensitive or insensitive, he didn't know.

"How about Monday night? New Year's Eve? Seven o'clock?"

"I—I don't—"

"Perfect night for a dinner date." Douglas had no idea if that was true. Restaurants were probably crowded on the last night of the year. Full of distractions, too. "Seven's the perfect time."

"Yeah, sure. I guess. We can talk about it later. I have to go. I—hey, put that down!"

She hung up without another word.

So, Douglas had a date for Monday night. On New Year's Eve. With Miranda.

And now that it was Monday, he was ready to collect on her agreement. After his lunch break had ended, he called her.

"Hey, Miranda," he said to her voicemail. "Just calling to remind you that we have a dinner planned tonight. Hope you'll be there."

He was about to hang up, but he stopped himself.

"I was thinking we could meet at Giovanni's Italian Delight. So, meet me there at seven. Okay, see you then."

He hung up and called Giovanni's to make his dinner reservation. Five minutes later, he called Miranda again.

"Hey, so let's not meet at Giovanni's. They're booked solid. Maybe Ferdinand's by the Sea would be better."

Five minutes later, he called her again.

"Hey Miranda, better make it Reggie's Pizza and Bowling Hut. We don't have to actually bowl."

Douglas hung up and cursed under his breath. What was he thinking trying to plan a dinner date with her on New Year's Eve? The only night that would've been worse was Valentine's Day. What was he even thinking?

Once work ended, he got in his car and drove home. On the way there, Miranda called him back.

"Hey, sorry about Saturday," she said. "I'll make it up to you. My friend's husband manages Nina's Sunshine Steakhouse. He can get us a table by the water. You can save your bowling shoes for another night with another woman."

Douglas slammed on his brakes. He was so distracted by his change in fortune that he'd almost plowed through a red light.

"Perfect," he said. "I will be sure to burn my bowling shoes as soon as I get home."

"Or you could just not wear them tonight. Wear some dress shoes instead."

"As you wish."

***

By 6:32, Douglas found an empty spot along the curb in front of a tea shop and parallel-parked his standard green two-door coupe between a golden BMV luxury sedan and a polished silver Sparky hybrid electric sports car, each of which had clearly been to the car wash several times since he'd last taken his in. As the lights of passing vehicles glittered off each car's respective paint job, those same lights diffused within Douglas's paint job, doing less to blind him, but also less to impress him.

Even though Miranda had already seen his car when she rode with him to the Olive Farm for lunch last week, she had not seen it in contrast with these other vehicles and, given the positive impression he wanted to have on her tonight, he hoped she never would. So, he hurried off the moment he locked his door. Because this spot was several blocks from the steakhouse, he didn't think she'd parked anywhere around here, but he didn't want to take the chance that she'd see him here, so he dissociated himself with his ugly car the first chance he got.

This, of course, meant he had to walk several blocks to reach the restaurant. But he didn't want to rush. Doing so would've raised his heart rate, and despite the chill of the evening on New Year's Eve in the suburbs of Chicago, he didn't want to make himself sweat. He'd wait for Miranda's line of questioning to cause him that discomfort.

On the way to the restaurant, he passed the usual array of boutiques and eateries, expecting most to be closed in anticipation of the New Year. Their dark entrances did not disappoint. But one shop caught his attention.

Ritzy and Respectable was a small designer jewelry shop halfway between two traffic lights, barely large enough for drivers or their passengers to notice, but just large enough for pedestrians to discover it. Even though there wasn't much business happening past the shop's windows, the lights were nevertheless on, and the sign on the door said it would be open late to ensure customers could look their best at midnight.

His instinct was to keep walking. Given his limited salary and even more limited budget, Douglas had decided long ago that he would spend money only on the items he needed when he needed them. And they had to be cheap. Extravagant expenses were never an option.

But this date was more important than his budget or his usual standards. Miranda was not just some rando he'd met on the internet during some late-night depression after he'd awoke at three in the morning alone and longing for company. No, Miranda was evergreen, a standout woman who exhibited a level of class, beauty, and quality that he could rarely find in anyone. To go into this date looking cheap and careless was unwise.

He considered his suit. His threads were pressed and stylish. But he lacked metal. A brass necklace or ring might have completed his look better. If Miranda was attracted to shiny objects, then he was foolish to walk away from the shop now.

Douglas checked his watch for the time, only to remind himself that he wasn't wearing a watch, and that his access to time was on his phone. To embody the complete picture of class and style, he wondered if it made sense to buy a watch, preferably one that matched the blue tweed jacket he wore under his dark heavy coat.

He checked his phone. Not much time to decide. If he wanted to make it his accessory of choice, he'd have to take his chances now and decide if it was worth it later.

So, he went inside to see what the shop offered.

And what he found was expensive.

Maybe he'd thought Ritzy and Respectable had a bargain bin section, but that's not what he found. The moment he checked the displays, he discovered just one section for watches and each watch glittering with gold or silver plating. No copper watches. No nickel plating. All for the same base cost.

The variances, however, were in the clock faces and hands—some faces reflected the light, and others absorbed it while some hands were crafted from diamonds and others from platinum or rubies—and, Douglas imagined, some varied in the craftsmanship. He had no doubt that each watch worked under the mechanical prowess of gears carved out of precious metals and diamond-encrusted lithium batteries. And the fobs—probably built from rare elastics, mined only from the ancient frozen jungles of Antarctica. Every part must've added another few hundred dollars to the bill. That must've been the explanation for the absurd prices.

Douglas was about to turn around and head for the door when the shopkeeper noticed him.

"Find what you're looking for, my dear?"

The bespectacled woman in her early thirties with cropped raven hair and dressed all in black approached him with sympathy in her eyes. She must've understood by looking at him that he could afford a new car sooner than he could afford one of these classy watches, and that he couldn't afford either now or ever.

"This one's nice," he said, pointing at a random watch without even looking at it.

The shopkeeper, Astrid, according to her glittering golden nametag, looked pleased.

"Ah, yes, our Divine Passage model. Ensure your last moments on earth are luxurious."

Douglas shivered at the sales pitch.

"Maybe that one," he said, pointing at another.

She nodded approvingly.

"You need a fine instrument to chronicle the final minutes of the year?" she asked.

Douglas shrugged. He wasn't even thinking about that.

"I just wanted to look nice for my date tonight."

"Ah." Astrid approached the watch display and checked the inventory for herself. "Must be an important date."

"You could say that."

"Perhaps you want our top-of-the-line model, look your absolute best."

"Preferably one that costs less than the price of my kidney?"

The shopkeeper frowned.

"I could recommend you another store. Have you heard of CostMart?"

"I should go. I'm going to be late."

Astrid reached for Douglas's shoulder.

"You say this date is important?"

"Very."

"Is it a matter of life and death?"

Douglas almost scoffed at the woman for her intense dramatic flair, but he stopped himself. No one had put a gun to his head to take Miranda to dinner, but he could see the motive didn't matter. He'd been thinking about her all week, every hour of every day, and the thought of her canceling or refusing to see him ever again made his stomach sick. No, it wasn't a matter of life and death, but it was a matter of happiness or misery. When his life was little more than fertilizer sales and collapses on the couch in front of terrible late night talk shows, the dread of existence tipped him closer to death. Miranda accepting him would bring him closer to life.

"Yeah, in a sense," he said.

"Then, perhaps I could interest you in another item, one a little more affordable." She narrowed her eyes at him. "Perhaps one more guaranteed to be a hit with your date, especially if the date goes well?"

Douglas faced her head-on.

"I'm listening."

She beckoned him to follow.

"Let me show you what we keep in the back room, what our usual clientele never sees."

Douglas's spine shook as he watched Astrid head for the back of the shop. She moved with shoulders straight but hips swaying, like a vertical plank shimmering as it glides down a motorized walkway. Everything about the woman's gothic looks and silky mannerisms told him he should run. But he checked his phone for the time instead. He still had twenty minutes to get to the restaurant.

Astrid approached the door to the back and opened it. She waited for him to follow. Curiosity was gnawing on his stomach. What could she possibly have back there that would impress Miranda so much?

There was only one way to find out.

Chapter 2

DOUGLAS HAD TO COVER his eyes with his forearm when he entered the back room of Ritzy and Respectable. The dazzling light reflecting off thousands of cut jewelry assaulted him like a strobe light. Between the blacklight effecting a gothic mood from above and the side panels' recessive lights shining high beams right into the display cases, Douglas's sense of light and dark did a cartwheel in his brain.

He'd barely gotten three feet in the door when he felt Astrid's delicate hand reaching under his elbow and digging into it with her claws.

"Come, follow me," she said, almost at a purr.

As the purple shade of sparkling ghostly insects dancing under his eyelids faded and normalized into a muddy brown nothing, Douglas dared to lower his arm and peek at the room before him. The lights were still mesmerizing, but now he could see the display cases in sharper relief.

And all around him were brooches that weighed down pockets, and bracelets that could scratch the skin off an attacker's face, and rings that could pick bank vault locks, and necklaces that must've been ripped right off a chandelier. The diamonds that glittered off each of their surfaces must've funded a thousand wars before they reached these exquisitely crafted objects. Douglas felt his soul sinking into the blackest dirt as he dared to step within inches of the nearest display.

He was so not worthy to stand here right now.

"You may find your night transform from average to greatness if you take one of these precious beauties to your date tonight."

Douglas almost put his fingers on the nearest glass case to steady himself, but he resisted. He just needed a look, a quick peek, a moment to soak in the intensity of the bracelets inside. Each one was a ring from Saturn fallen from space. The shopkeeper stood poised beside it, her blood red lipstick contrasting sharply with the black dress that absorbed every light that hit it. She looked as if she were balancing on a crystal bowling ball, keeping steady on the impossible. It was only then that Douglas noticed she had rubies etched into her six-inch stiletto heels.

The upscale Victorian glamor raised in value every second he stared at anything. He was wise to run.

But he didn't. He was paralyzed.

"Could I interest you in the Giardino Magnifique?"

"The what?"

Astrid dug her fingernails under the display lid and raised the glass just high enough to reach inside. She lifted out a bracelet about four inches in diameter, with an elastic band made of silk and titanium, and amber-colored jewels that were so clear that Douglas could see right through to her fingers.

"Mined from the depths of the Himalayas and crafted in the workshops of Kathmandu, this lovely specimen will charm the pants off any stubborn partner or client."

"I—"

"Or maybe you'd prefer the Anastasia Maxima." Astrid set the bracelet with the Italian-French name from Kathmandu back on its perch and retrieved another bracelet, this one blue as sapphire and shimmering as the ocean. "Dating back to the fourteen hundreds, the Anastasia Maxima is the jewel of Czechoslovakia."

If his college world history class hadn't lied to him, then Douglas was pretty certain Czechoslovakia had formed at the end of World War I, not the fifteenth century, but he wasn't about to debate the shopkeeper about history. The bracelet was truly a wonder to behold.

"Imagine your lovely date—what is her name?"

"Mir—Miranda."

"Imagine Mirmiranda adorned in the Anastasia. Wondrous, isn't it?"

Douglas was ready to agree, but he didn't know what Miranda was wearing tonight. It was possible the intense blue would clash with her dress, or shoes, or even her hair. How was he supposed to know?

"I'm not sure if—"

"Oh, or maybe you'd prefer something more noticeable. Could I interest you in a necklace? Perhaps the Poison Flame?"

"I—wait, the poison what?"

Astrid led him to another display and pointed at a heavy chain made of the richest jade. Each link had a diamond hanging from it on a silvery thread.

"Behold the crown jewel of the Everglades, perfect for your southern belle who needs that taste of her sultry homeland in this dark winter wasteland."

Douglas couldn't help but wonder if the necklace was too heavy.

"How much does it cost?"

Astrid snatched his wrists from his sides and held them firm in her cold palms.

"My dear, my sweet naïve dear. What is the price of love?"

"Depends on how much this costs."

"If you want to be a hit with your Mirmiranda, then you must show her, prove to her that she is worth her weight in gold. In fact . . ." Astrid pulled Douglas along to the next display. Inside was a collection of golden earrings. Most looked normal, save for the splatter of glimmering red peeking through the gold like sunspots. "Ancient royal earrings straight from tenth century Cairo. Legend has it Cleopatra's youngest sister wore these earrings on her wedding day."

Douglas had heard nothing of Cleopatra's siblings, but maybe Astrid was better educated than he was.

"Okay, how much?"

Astrid clucked her tongue and shook her head. Her face was now serious. She couldn't have been over thirty or thirty-five, but she suddenly looked sixty.

"You ask questions that do not respect the privilege you have here tonight. What is your name?"

"Douglas."

"Douglas, let me ask you the most important question you will ever hear. What value is a dollar if you lose out on precious time?"

"A dollar."

"A lifetime, Douglas. A lifetime."

Astrid pulled him along to another display, this time full of diamond rings.

"Do you love this woman, Douglas?"

"I'm not—"

She tugged on his wrists harder.

"Do you *not* love this woman?"

"It's a bit early to—"

"It's now or never, Douglas. Your future depends on the decision you make tonight. Do you love Mirmiranda?"

"I mean, we just met and—"

"Love does not wait for your procrastination, Douglas. Nor does it respect your feelings or lack thereof. Love is real, and you love this woman. I can tell. It's in your eyes."

"I—"

"Yes, your eyes. Both of them. Even as you twitch, I can tell."

"But I—"

"You came to me for a reason, Douglas, and I brought you here so that you don't waste the one and only opportunity you will ever have at true love. You must not waste it."

Douglas was nearly ready to protest, but Astrid's face had gone soft. Her eyes had begun to flutter. Her fingers caressed his wrists with softness.

"Why make Mirmiranda suffer through your indecision? Why even have indecision? Isn't she the one you want?"

"I mean—"

Astrid flung Douglas's wrists out of her hands, and she promptly turned her back to him. Once again, her youthful shape took prominence, and Douglas couldn't help but wonder for a moment what she might look like undressed.

"Then why date her, Douglas? If you do not love her, then why waste her time?"

"I just want to—"

Astrid wheeled on him.

"You are wasting her time." Her index finger was practically in his face. But again, she softened. She lowered it to his chest, then rested her palm on him. "Perhaps you might prefer a woman like me instead?"

Douglas hesitated. Astrid had a pleasant touch, but—

"But perhaps not," she said, her face moving through emotions as the seasons might change in a time lapsed video. "Perhaps you would think of her, even as you lay with me."

"I don't—"

"You are being unfair to both of us, Douglas. And to yourself." Astrid reached into the display and propped a diamond ring just large enough to fit an average-sized woman's finger right before his face. "Give her this ring. Tonight." Astrid's face was deadly serious now. "You will not regret it. I promise you."

"It just seems so—"

Astrid reached down and placed the ring in his palm. It was certainly sturdy.

"Important?" she said, finishing his sentence.

Douglas couldn't tell if she'd even looked at the ring she was showing him. But something about it did feel right sitting in the palm of his hand.

"I was gonna say—"

"That your beautiful future wife will love this gift? Yes, I already know. That is why I am offering to give it to you for next to nothing."

Douglas stiffened.

"Really?"

"You have until I reach the register to claim it for yourself at the special price I am giving you. If you are not there with me by the time I look back, this special offer goes away forever, and with it, all hope for happiness."

Douglas felt a sharp tension overcoming him. He didn't want to miss out on happiness. He already had so little of it that he—wait a minute.

"Are you playing me right now?"

Astrid strutted past him, emphasizing the shake in her hips. She was the kind of woman that casting directors often chose for the role of femme fatale in those old 1940s detective movies.

"Tick tock, Douglas. Your opportunity is about to end."

Douglas stared at the ring. It reflected every light in the room back at him.

What if Astrid had a point?

And what if he was about to waste the opportunity of a lifetime debating the matters of the heart against reason?

Astrid reached the door back to the main showroom. He was about to miss his chance at happiness forever.

"Wait up," he said.

***

After Douglas stuffed the plastic bag from Ritzy and Respectable under his coat, he ran out the door and dashed for the next intersection. It probably wasn't a good look running from a jewelry shop with an item concealed under his clothes, but he couldn't worry about that now. According to the time, he had five minutes to get to the steakhouse.

Good thing his wallet was much lighter now. Less cash to slow him down. Unfortunately, "less expensive" didn't mean "cheap." Or "less expensive." More like, "Symbolically less expensive, assuming you get the result you want."

When he finally got to Nina's Sunshine Steakhouse, he was out of breath, and his heart was racing. But he was also relieved. Miranda had yet to arrive. He was two minutes late, so she was also two minutes late.

Douglas let the host know he was here and that he was still waiting for his party. The host told him his table was being prepared. Meanwhile, he checked inside his coat pocket for the special gift he'd bought and confirmed it hadn't fallen out on the way over. With everything aligned, he could relax now.

At 7:10, Douglas watched every car that found a spot along the curb or at the valet station, and he studied each woman that stepped out. By 7:15, he checked his phone for any missed calls. There were none. At 7:20, he once again checked his coat for the plastic bag containing the special gift, hoping he could still pass it along tonight.

"Sir, your table is ready," the host said. "Has your party arrived?"

"Not yet. But she'll be here."

He hoped he was telling the truth.

The steakhouse was crowded tonight. As the host led him through the dining room toward the deck area where his table sat, Douglas noted each patron he passed, making sure Miranda hadn't snuck in ahead of him and spent the last twenty minutes waiting for nothing. Most were older than he was, or classier, or both. All were dressed in formalwear, likely their best, or their better, or their usual. Some were likely heads of companies, but others were probably museum owners, or heirs to thrones, or . . .

Douglas's coworkers.

Douglas pressed his palm to his face and hurried off to his table, hoping they wouldn't see him. He didn't like talking to them at work, so he certainly didn't want to talk to them here. Once the host seated him at his table between a heater and the icy lake, Douglas peeked into the dining room to ensure no one had spotted him.

"Could I start you off with a glass of wine?" the host asked.

His coworkers remained seated, already engaged in whatever conversations they were having, laughing at whatever stupid jokes they were making. They hadn't noticed him. And as long as they kept their focus on each other, they were unlikely to spot him sitting alone on the deck by the water, in the cold.

Douglas nodded.

"I'll have your signature red."

"Very good, sir."

The host hurried off. Douglas checked his phone. Miranda still hadn't called. And she was almost half an hour late.

He covered his eyes with his hands. He hoped he hadn't made a mistake coming here tonight. And the weight of the plastic bag sitting on his abdomen reminded him of the costly error he'd made stopping by Ritzy and Respectable if she weren't coming tonight. Even if the item were refundable, his shame and foolishness certainly wouldn't be.

The host brought him an empty goblet and a bottle of Exquisite Squeeze signature red wine and poured the glass half full. Douglas downed the whole thing in a single gulp.

"Sir?"

Douglas gestured at him to pour him another.

"Very good. Tastes like cherries or whatever. Another, please."

The host poured him another. Douglas just took a sip this time.

"Yeah, okay. You can leave the bottle. But bring a second glass. I know she'll be here."

"But of course."

The host brought the second glass, then assured him the server would arrive shortly. Douglas told him not to bother until his date arrived. The host bowed in acceptance.

So, Douglas was left alone again, with two goblets, a bottle of wine, and still no date.

His coworkers, meanwhile, were smirking at each other's company. He wondered if they were going home with each other tonight.

The thought of it made him take another sip of his wine. And another.

Chapter 3

Douglas felt a tap on his shoulder. It was at that moment he realized he'd fallen asleep on the table. He'd downed four half goblets of wine over the course of ten minutes, and the sudden spike in alcohol must've knocked him out. He was about to sit up and apologize to the host for napping on the patio when he watched the feminine hand with the pink fingernails skim off his shoulder and toward the chair opposite his. He sat up just in time to watch Miranda sit down.

"So sorry I'm late," she said, when she slid herself forward, closing the gap between the table and her sternum. "Had an emergency."

"You seem to have a lot of those."

"Comes with the territory."

Douglas was fighting to see her, as sleep and alcohol—he imagined—had dulled the clarity of his vision. But Miranda was there, for real, and looking as lovely as he'd hoped she would. She arrived wearing a velvet coat and an attractive red dress underneath, with a silver broach above her left breast and a matching necklace coming off her collarbone. Her dark hair was rolled into a double-knotted ponytail with a pink pin sticking through it. She was also wearing lipstick that matched her dress and eyeshadow that matched the winter season.

So, she was clearly trying to look nice tonight. Maybe the emergency really was an issue, and maybe she had legitimately tried to get here on time.

So, maybe Douglas wouldn't make a big deal about it, or even check the time—

It was 7:48. He justified looking at his phone to see if she'd left him a message. She hadn't.

"How come you didn't call?"

Miranda leaned forward and reached out for his hand.

"I would have. But I was driving. All over town."

"You didn't have stop lights?"

She straightened herself out, grabbed her goblet, poured herself a glass of wine.

"I assume this is for us." She took a sip and melted at the taste. "Perfect."

She set her glass down as she savored what was in her mouth. Once she swallowed, she answered Douglas's question.

"I had plenty. But I'm not that person who makes or takes calls at lights. It'll eventually turn green."

"So, what was the emergency?"

"Same thing it always is."

"Which is?"

"Personal."

Douglas nodded. So, that was the score so far. Mystery, one; Illumination, zero.

"Well, you look nice," Douglas said, wrestling the line of discussion back to something date-worthy.

"As do you. Have you ordered yet?"

Douglas caught Miranda up on the state of the evening so far. The host had brought him wine and instructed the server to stay away until the man's second party member arrived. Now that she was here, the server was likely to swoop in and save dinner.

Miranda unfolded her napkin and set it on her lap. As she made her adjustments, she glanced over her shoulder into the main dining room on the other side of the glass. One table in particular caught her attention.

"Hey, isn't that the woman I'd tried and failed selling my books to last week?"

She was staring at the table with Douglas's coworkers enjoying a lobster together. He nodded.

"Yep, that's Angela, the woman who steers our ship of fools, the queen of fertilizer, the master of our dungeon."

"She's married?"

Douglas laughed—couldn't stop himself.

"No, that's not her husband. Maybe not even her boyfriend. That's Winston, the guy who bought me the basketball tickets for Secret Santa. I don't know what to make of that scenario."

Miranda looked impressed.

"I did not take her as the type who could keep a man."

"Again, not sure that's the situation. Knowing Angela, she's probably bribing him to work fifty hours next week, though I wouldn't know why. She's supposed to be on vacation now. Maybe that's why. Lobster might be his payment."

"Well, they don't make a cute couple at any rate."

Angela Prince, for all her professional venom, was still an attractive woman aesthetically, with her long blonde hair, fit body, and general good taste in clothing. And Winston, a bit of a waif and male wallflower, still wore his glasses and 1980s rocker face stubble like a champ. Physically speaking, they didn't make an ugly couple. But Douglas saw Miranda's point. They looked like two people who wouldn't normally enjoy each other's company. And, as far as Douglas knew, the look matched the reality. Winston usually kept to himself, and his resistance to responding to any of Angela's comments, which she likely made as a person of many opinions despite her company, reflected that. The smile on his face suggested that maybe he liked listening to her, but it could've also suggested that he liked lobster. The evidence was unclear.

Then again, at the end of the Christmas party, Angela had claimed to help Winston with the cost of the basketball tickets. Why else would she have helped him pay for it if they weren't secretly seeing each other? That question had haunted Douglas for the last week. If the reality was that they were in fact seeing each other, then maybe they did enjoy each other's company, and that didn't make Douglas feel any better. It meant he couldn't borrow anything else from Winston's desk without asking for it, for fear the boss might get involved.

"Wow, that sucks," Douglas said.

"What?"

Douglas shook his head. He was thinking out loud again.

"Nothing. So, here we are. Two better-looking people on a more sensible date. Tell me something about you I don't know."

"You don't know anything, so the field is wide."

"Surprise me. Tell me about growing up. Or maybe start with high school. Or perhaps—"

Before Douglas could finish, the server arrived with the menus. So, in classic first date fashion, the rolling conversation was just about to hit its stride when the interruptions began. He supposed this would set the pace for the evening.

He smiled when he took the menu. After wasting the mustachioed server's time for forty-five minutes, he figured the smile was fair play for having the tuxedo-clad man interrupt his conversation with this beautiful woman.

The conversation would have to regain momentum after the drinks were served.

The drinks were served. Miranda told Douglas about her interest in nursing as a career, starting at the beginning with her enrollment in nursing school and backtracking to why she wanted to sign up in the first place.

He fought his urge to yawn at her story. But he listened and nodded, anyway. At present, she was a salesgirl for a local publishing company who offered custom-made books and brochures to businesses who wanted to expand their reach by sharing detailed information to prospecting customers. But sales literature wasn't her passion. Her passion was in helping people, especially those on the brink of death. Her passion turned to borderline obsession, and one day she showed up on campus to the local community college and signed up.

"I'm almost finished with my classes," she said. "Just one semester left, and that's mainly onsite at the hospital."

Douglas covered his mouth with his hand. He could stop himself from yawning openly, but he couldn't stop the strain in his jaw from a clandestine yawn.

"So, what are you going to do about your brochures if you're at the hospital every day?" he asked, hoping to mask his boredom with the topic.

"Work weekends."

Douglas smiled. Such an obvious answer. He'd forgotten what it was like to work hard at achieving a goal.

"Any thought to what happens once you change careers?" he asked.

"Well, sure. I start a new life."

"Around here?"

"Hopefully. I have a house. I'd like to keep living in it."

Douglas moved his hand closer to hers, but he stopped himself from taking it. The night and their conversation were warming, but he wasn't about to lose the evening on poor impulse control, not if he could help it.

"Any thought to how it might affect your social life?"

"Sure."

Douglas waited for her to finish her thought, but it was apparently finished. Then he noticed the glimmer, the twinkle in her eyes. She was teasing him now.

"Any room for special company amid this career shift?" he asked.

"Might be difficult. But not impossible." She thought about her answer. "Depends how tired I am at midnight."

Douglas felt something skip either in his heart or his crotch. He couldn't pinpoint the origin since it hit him so fast. Midnight socials had so many possibilities. Nothing to yawn at there.

Rather than embarrass himself with an inappropriate follow-up question, however, he took a sip of wine.

Meanwhile, out of the corner of his eye, he noticed Angela laughing at something Winston had said to her. The fact that she'd laugh at anything also caught him by surprise. Usually, she'd smirk with patronizing disdain embedded underneath her lips.

Either she was playing Winston for a fool, or she genuinely found amusement in his words. With Angela, it was so hard to tell.

Normally, Douglas would've kept the conversation on its current course and let it run to its natural end. But he couldn't help but comment on the anomaly he was witnessing in real-time. Not saying anything about it had the same effect on him as passing a road accident and pretending it never happened.

"You ever wonder why two boring and incompatible people might have dinner together on New Year's Eve?" Douglas asked.

"I'm not boring," Miranda said, her tone suddenly harsh.

Douglas shook his head and grabbed her hand.

"No, no, not us." He pointed at his coworkers' table. "Them."

Miranda followed his gaze and shrugged.

"Maybe they don't find each other boring."

"But could you imagine? What if they got married? Had kids? What would their conversations be like? 'Honey, I paid the electric bill today.' 'That's great, honey. I put gas in the car.' 'Oh, that's wonderful, honey. Wanna have sex?' 'Sure, but maybe after the evening news.' 'Great, I'll warm up the soup.' How depressing."

"They could just be out on a business dinner, like you'd suggested."

"Yeah, but on New Year's Eve? I don't know. I think I'm bothered by this."

"You have a thing for your boss?"

"No, I mean I think the world is in danger of exploding because clearly the forces of normality are severely challenged tonight, and we should all be worried by this pairing."

"We don't have to talk about them if you don't want. Sorry I was late, but I'm here now. We can talk about us instead. If you want."

"Sorry, I'm just—what am I missing here? I mean, I'm sure they have their merits. Angela doesn't wear Dalmatian puppy fur, far as I know. Maybe Winston is the secret guitarist of a long-forgotten rock band. Why waste the evening—"

"Again, I think two people can enjoy each other's company for any reason, even if you don't understand it. And the world doesn't have to end because of it."

He glanced at her and smiled.

"Is this your way of saying you enjoy my company?"

Miranda noticed he was holding her hand and slipped out from his grip.

"The night is still young, and we've barely shared a single interesting thing about each other."

Douglas fought the urge to claim they had yet to share *any* interesting thing about each other.

"So, tell me something interesting about you," he said.

Miranda winked. "You first."

Douglas leaned back in his seat, suddenly aware that he was on the spot. What was interesting about him? He hadn't given it much thought before now.

"I'm good at predicting the future," he said after a moment's thought.

"Yeah, give me an example."

His neck throbbed. How was he supposed to give an example? The future hadn't happened yet, and any existing example would take setting up and paying off. And he didn't think Miranda would be interested in hearing about his prediction that Sam Trowel would vomit all over himself after binge-consuming beer and chips in the office lunchroom on a rather dark Tuesday a few months ago after conducting a particularly bad sales pitch to a particularly important client.

Douglas sipped his wine. He'd just have to make something up. How would Miranda know the difference if she, herself, couldn't project herself through time and space?

"Sure." He cleared his throat and pointed at the table of coworkers he wished he had the power to ignore. "Take two people on a date, for example. Two people like Angela and Winston. Or two people like us. Imagine a world where that date becomes a happy marriage."

"This the future or a fantasy?"

"Let's figure that out later. First, imagine Winston getting down on one knee and proposing to Angela, and Angela stealing the ring out of his hand and declaring with great happiness a resounding 'yes,' assuming she isn't excited just because she could get good money for the ring."

"How romantic a thought."

"Then imagine they have an extravagant wedding where their combined total of a dozen friends shows up to celebrate."

"In the future."

"Yes, in the future. Imagine they are the only two people in the world who could possibly love each other, so, of course, this marriage would work beautifully. Or maybe that's our story since the future is still untold."

"But for now let's pretend it's Winston and Angela's story."

Douglas sipped his wine. She'd sensed his subversiveness, it seemed. Smart woman.

"Yes, about Winston, Angela, and their 'happily ever after.'"

"Or their 'happily for now.'"

Very smart woman.

Happy New Life

Tᴴᴱ ʜᴏɴᴇʏᴍᴏᴏɴ ʜᴀᴅ ᴄᴏᴍᴇ to a satisfying conclusion. After a few nice breakfasts and several sessions of mediocre sex that didn't need discussion or introspection, Winston and Angela returned to Winston's apartment to gather the last of his boxes. They were in the final stages of moving his stuff into Angela's suburban home where Winston could finally enjoy having a backyard of his own—along with Angela—and their happy new life could begin officially once they got those final boxes unpacked, hopefully by the next day.

Winston had spent years living in this seedy building with the peeling wallpaper and apathetic landlord, scraping by on his existence, affording only the necessities after paying his overpriced rent and electric to the man. But now he could escape the landlord's clutches, falling instead into Angela's hopefully softer claws that demanded less for rent and more for investments, including what remained of her mortgage. Her grip would still be greedy, of course, but the benefits she'd provide him for his payments were far better. Or at least somewhat better.

For one, living with Angela meant Winston could upgrade his home from a single bedroom, single bathroom, and eight-by-eight living room and kitchen respectively to a house double in size, plus an extra bedroom for an office, and a back porch for entertaining, now that he could afford to have friends.

It also meant having a two-car garage and laundry room, allowing him to protect his vehicle from vandals and his laundry from Laundromat theft. He'd also have more room for keeping food in a pantry and space for a larger refrigerator, which Angela had already paid for and installed. And with the living room having an extra twelve feet on every side, Winston could finally sit on a full-sized couch and watch his favorite movies on a 55-inch television, both of which Angela had already owned.

But then there were the financial benefits. Angela would still want to keep her own separate bank account on top of having access to his, but the joint account they could now establish meant his expenses would become more manageable. He made enough in his position at the fertilizer company to get by on his own, but Angela's salary was almost three times higher, making their joint account at least fifty percent more flexible with bills and lifestyle needs, giving him more room to breathe.

So, marrying Angela certainly relieved him of his money burdens.

But then there was also the social element. Neither Winston nor Angela had many friends—if any—but now they had each other. When Winston lived alone, he had the displeasure of listening to his neighbors on the left scream at each other over things like throwing out the trash and leaving the toilet seat down, while his neighbors on the right spent too much time screaming in delight as their furniture bumped into the wall in increasingly rhythmic fury. And sometimes his neighbors on both sides exchanged heated threats with each other, through his walls, over how distracting their angry arguments over trash and toilet seats clashed with their angry bouts of bed-thumping against the wall.

Getting out of his apartment meant losing those neighbors, but it also meant losing his landlord. His landlord, a former tech tycoon who'd gotten addicted to painkillers, raised the rent by twenty dollars every month, and he'd threaten Winston with an eviction notice every time he asked him to stabilize it. It had gotten to the point where the landlord would appear at his doorstep every Saturday, a plastic cup of scotch and opiates in one hand and an eviction notice with an updated countdown if new fees were not paid by the end of the month in the other, threatening to send his lawyers and an auction house after him if he didn't have every cent he'd asked for. It was certainly no one he'd call a friend.

None of them were anyone he'd consider a friend.

So, moving into Angela's home also meant he'd get to live with someone who said she liked him. It also meant getting to have romantic evenings with a decent-looking woman, if romantic evenings with Angela was the sort of thing a man wanted, which Winston clearly did for some reason.

Once Winston carried his last few boxes of mementos out of this rat-infested, roach-infested apartment, he closed this chapter of his life forever and started his new one. The moment he dropped these same boxes on the floor of the spare bedroom-office and unpacked them, checking for any stowaway rats or roaches that hadn't jumped ship in transit, feeling relief that he didn't find any, Winston sat behind his new desk and closed his eyes.

Their happy new life had officially begun.

Then he opened his eyes and stared at the wall. He realized he didn't know what that meant.

But that was okay. He was here now, in the home that he would now and forever consider the place where he kept his stuff, the place where he could freely walk around with his pants unbuttoned and no one would notice, the place where he could see the same woman day after day and think, *Yeah, that's no dream. She's real.* This was the place where dreams came true, or at least where a few dreams came true, certainly where his old dreams couldn't completely die. Tonight, he was living his first dream.

He opened his desk drawers to find them empty. Now it was time to fill them with memories, or more specifically, it was time to fill them with pens and reams of paper. The last time he'd tried this in a place he'd called home, a leak in the ceiling from an upstairs neighbor's overflowing toilet ruined his desk. But that wouldn't happen here. Angela owned a one-story house.

"Would you like a muffin for lunch?" Angela whispered through the office door.

Before getting married, Winston would have to get his own muffins. Now, as a married man, he not only had the woman of his dreams—if Angela were the kind of woman men dreamed about—but he also had lunch served to him on a platter, or at least on a plate.

"Yes, Muffin." Winston noticed the irony of his pet name for his new wife after she'd walked away.

A few minutes later, Angela entered the office with a small poppyseed fun-sized muffin on a napkin. She set it on the desk before him, then tapped on his nose as she wiggled hers.

"Enjoy it, you stud muffin."

Back in real life, Miranda had to stop Douglas there.

"Are they really going to use so many puns in their relationship?" she asked.

Douglas shrugged. "Why wouldn't they?"

She shook her head.

"No offense to your coworkers, but they sound like they have an awful life."

"Well, yeah, but marriage is great, even for sad sacks like them. Right?"

"Debatable. When does their life get more interesting?"

"I don't know. They think it's interesting. That's what matters. Winston gets to enjoy a bigger bedroom, and a kitchen, and a—"

"What does Angela get to enjoy?"

"Whatever Winston brings to the table."

"Which is?"

Douglas was about to continue his story, but he stopped himself before the first word left his mouth.

"Okay, maybe they're the wrong example. Let's consider a different couple." He took a sip of his drink. "Maybe we'll consider ourselves, assuming this date leads to another one."

Miranda placed her chin on her fist and smiled. "Yes, please tell me more about *our* future, assuming we have one."

Douglas cracked his knuckles and gave himself a moment to wash out any visual that might've floated around in his head about Winston and Angela enjoying the pleasures of married life. His solution was to mentally put his face over Winston's face and Miranda's over Angela's. He also imagined being in a different house, with different décor and room options, and different furniture. In Douglas's fantasy, his couch faced a 75-inch television, and Miranda walked around in lingerie all hours of the day.

"You sure you want to hear this?"

"Of course I do. How else will I know if I should be here tonight?"

Douglas gave her a double take. It sounded like she was testing him.

"Of course you should be here tonight. You are here."

She gestured him to continue. "Great. Go on, I want to hear this."

Douglas took a breath. Every first date guaranteed at least one obstacle between the parties involved and a lifetime of happiness. That obstacle usually came in the form of unintentional idiocy, often through the vehicle of stupid opinions. That vehicle had been Douglas's downfall many times before, and somehow it had always caught him when his guard was down.

The conversation officially hit the starting gate to that possible nightmare scenario when Miranda leaned forward to offer him her full attention. So, he had to tread carefully here, ensuring his guard was up this time. But he also had to consider that Miranda was toying with him. She probably wanted to hear his creativity, if not his honesty regarding the future of their relationship, assuming they had one. Either way, he assumed she was offering him some wiggle room to say the wrong thing with the right intentions.

Then again, he'd assumed that before with the other women.

Of course, in the past, he hadn't noticed the expressions on his dates' faces, even if he'd seen them. Fuzzy recollection of their memory ghosts revealed more serious looks, however, looks similar to what he'd seen on Angela's face day after day. This time, he noticed the light amusement on Miranda's face. Maybe she wanted an uncensored story, or just a funny one. To offer her a sanitized version would've likely smelled like cheese.

She gestured him again when he said nothing. So, the starting gate opened, and he was off.

"Right. It starts with you bringing me eggs and waffles for breakfast, not lunch."

"No muffins?"

"Well, you could always bring me muffins. Those go well with breakfast."

"What am I bringing you for lunch?"

"Treats. Meats. Sweets. You-name-it."

"What are you making me for dinner?" Miranda's eyes twinkled at the question.

"What am I making you?" Douglas took another sip of his drink. He wasn't prepared for such an outrageous question. He was no cook.

Miranda closed her eyes and nodded.

"If I'm bringing you breakfast and lunch," she said, "what are you bringing me for dinner?"

Douglas glanced around the room beyond the glass. The restaurant was lively tonight, with servers hopping to and from every table, hand-delivering all sorts of steamy plates of exciting foods. The moment was too obvious to ignore. He outstretched his hands to show off his solution.

"I'm bringing you here for dinner, of course."

Miranda sipped her drink, her smile now faded.

"Of course you are," she said.

Douglas twiddled his thumbs as he watched her swallow her drink, her face now expressionless. Apparently, he'd tripped over the first obstacle.

After a moment of uncomfortable silence, he dared to ask the question he didn't want to ask. "Is that not what you'd want?"

Miranda shrugged. "This place is nice. I like it enough. But not every night."

"Then I can take you to another restaurant."

"Or you could make me dinner at home."

Douglas glanced at the lake off the patio deck. What did he know about cooking for another human being?

"What would you like?"

"Whatever you decide to make."

Another moment of silence passed between them.

Mercifully, the server returned with the appetizers. The guy distracted them with the usual nonsense banter that servers generally offer desperate men who have clearly stepped in a pool of mud with whatever stupid topic of discussion they've introduced or unsuccessfully navigated through, giving Douglas an excuse to pretend that line of conversation is over, and a new one should find its way into their mouths.

"And that's why I like the special," the server said, finishing his brief journey into a tangent. "So, if you have room tonight, I'd recommend it."

"Sounds lovely, thank you," Miranda said. When the server left, she returned her focus to Douglas. "Would you make me the special for dinner?"

Okay, so this topic wasn't about to die. He'd have to address it. Now he remembered why he'd stopped dating women he didn't know.

"I don't know how to cook anything that doesn't involve chicken or noodles," he said.

Miranda winked at him. "I knew it."

"Is that a deal-breaker?"

Miranda sipped her drink as she held his gaze. When she finished, she pushed her glass aside and leaned back in her seat.

"I derailed you. Finish your story. What's your idea of the perfect future with me?"

Douglas felt his neck tighten. After getting the lukewarm grilling on whether he'd make her dinner, perhaps ever, he worried he'd step in more hot water, trip over more obstacles. Maybe the amusing route wasn't the right path through this topic.

"What would you like our perfect future to be?" he asked, deciding he didn't want to think in the wrong direction about this any further.

Miranda smiled.

"That's a good question. Maybe I'll save that answer for the end of the night, assuming we get that far."

Douglas drank his water to cool down his neck. This sounded like the dangerous territory was expanding.

"In the meantime," Miranda said, "I'd like you to finish your story. What does our perfect future look like?"

Douglas sighed. She wasn't about to let go. So, he continued the story, this time swapping Winston and Angela out with himself and Miranda.

Miranda entered the office in her very conservative, in no way revealing pajamas, the ones that came with pants and a jacket (and also some socks). She was as beautiful without makeup as she was with—

"Okay," Miranda said, interrupting his story. "I know that's not how you think."

"Of course it is," Douglas lied. "Why would I tell you any differently?"

Miranda took his hand.

"Here, let me help you out. It's eight o'clock in the morning, you're in your office, and I enter fully made-up and completely naked. And I'm bringing you waffles. Now what?"

Douglas opened his mouth, ready to take the line she'd fed him, but popped a chip in it instead. Whether this was a trap or not, he wasn't about to fall for it. No one ever set this line of conversation on a first date without trying to sabotage it, not in his experience, at least.

Once he swallowed his chip, he followed it with water, cleared his throat, and smiled.

"That's not my perfect marriage," he said.

Miranda gave him a stern look.

"Come now. You started our relationship with a lie. Are you seriously going to drop me another one so soon?"

"No, I'm telling you the truth. You're wearing pajamas. But the waffles sound pretty great."

Miranda cocked her head sideways. She clearly didn't believe him.

"See," Douglas continued, "if you present yourself at your very best first thing in the morning, what does that save for the evening? In our perfect marriage, you would *end* the night naked with waffles, not starting it."

Miranda bit her lower lip and squeezed his hand. Then her grip tightened. And tightened some more. Douglas suddenly felt the urge to shake her loose.

"But I'd be equally happy with just a regular evening watching television with my wife," he said, pulling himself free. "Pants on and everything."

"Mind if I tell you what I think your coworkers' future marriage would look like?"

"Ugh, you're not going to be dirty about it, are you?"

Miranda couldn't help but laugh at his comment. Maybe that was a no.

"My story will be far more realistic," she said.

"Yeah, all right. Let me hear your ideas."

"Because Winston's such a waif, I'll have to reverse their usual roles."

"Do what you must."

Miranda cracked her knuckles. So, she had a flair for the dramatic also.

"It begins with Angela wearing all black."

New Fear's Eve

As the clock struck midnight, Angela pecked her new husband, Winston, on the cheek. That was good enough. No sense in overdoing it tonight. A new year didn't equate to false hope. Why make her new husband think he'd get lucky tonight? That wasn't the precedent she wanted to set for the year, nor was it a thought she wanted planted in Winston's mind. A kiss on the cheek was good enough to say, "I love you," without saying, "I want you." The new year needed to start off right, and that meant setting the proper expectations.

Winston, in all his horniness, returned the kiss on the cheek. Angela pushed him off when he lingered on her skin for more than a second.

"Save something for Valentine's Day," she said.

Angela stalked off with Winston's lips still puckered where her cheek had been and headed for the table of wine glasses. Dressed in all black, she was careful not to stain any of it in red.

Meanwhile, in the corner of the party room where everyone in the office had gathered, the security guard was swaying from side-to-side to the music, watching Angela's and Winston's every move. As Angela took a sip of wine, she noticed the guard staring at her. She tipped her glass in his direction.

He looked the other way, turning his attention to someone else instead.

Winston edged up to his new wife once her glass was empty. She'd established a rule earlier that evening that he was to keep his distance while she drank. She didn't want him commenting on her wine habits or daring to sneak a sip or anything. Just because they were married now didn't mean they had to do everything together. In fact, Angela preferred that they did most things separately.

"I think better when you're not around," was her excuse.

Winston had no choice but to agree. Before they started dating, Angela would often shoo him away whenever he had an accounting question or a concern about safety or anything that took her from her thoughts. Getting married wasn't likely to change any of that, at least not right away, or at least not with the likelihood of things returning to the old way after some time had passed.

Winston found a chair at the other side of the room and drank his flat flute of champaign. Angela, meanwhile, went talking to the office secretary. In the middle of the conversation, the security guard marched over and started talking smoothly.

"Nice dress," he said to her.

"It won't be on forever," she replied, following it with a sip of wine.

"I'd like to be there when it comes off."

Angela smirked at him.

"I'm married now."

"That wasn't your excuse last week."

Douglas had to stop Miranda before she started her next sentence.

"Nobody wants to have an affair with Angela," he said. "And you accuse me of lying."

"Well, I don't know these people. What's the security guard's name?"

"Harvey."

"In my story, Harvey and Angela are seeing each other behind Winston's and Fiona's back."

"Who's Fiona?"

"Harvey's wife."

"That's not his wife's name."

"Doesn't matter. In my story, he's married to Fiona. So, Angela and Harvey are seeing each other behind Winston's and Fiona's back."

"Why?"

"Because it's more dramatic."

"I thought this was about the perfect marriage."

"If that little mousy guy was her husband, wouldn't she be happier with the big security guard?"

Douglas considered her rationale. While he liked Winston as a human being, he couldn't help but notice he was a bit on the weak side, maybe even spineless. And he probably would kiss Angela exactly the way Miranda had described it.

But this was an unfair assessment. Winston deserved Angela cheating on him as much as he deserved her marrying him.

"Let's leave the affairs out of the story," Douglas said. "Let's pretend their marriage is functional."

Miranda took a bite of her food.

"Like I said, I don't know these people. I'm just telling you how marriage works."

"By setting up an affair?"

Miranda washed her food down with water.

"Some marriages are tainted with affairs," she said. "What makes Winston and Angela's any different?"

Douglas didn't have an answer for her. As before when he had nothing to say, his attention drifted off to the lake. For some reason, he was expecting to see ducks out there, but it was probably too cold for that.

"So, Harvey took her rebuff lightly. Even as she pretended she wasn't interested, her skin shivered as Harvey's eyes moved down her back and to her hips. They both licked their lips simultaneously."

"Gross," Douglas said.

When the party was over and they headed home to Angela's house, now also Winston's house, Angela checked her phone for messages. Three of her old college friends had wished her a Happy New Year, and Harvey had left her a picture of his genitals. She deleted it before Winston could look over and see it.

"Okay, I don't want to hear this story anymore," Douglas said. "I'd asked you to keep it clean."

"I never agreed to that."

"Maybe we should change the subject."

"Aw, don't you want to hear a romantic story about two married people?"

"No."

Miranda's stiff composure crumbled. She burst out laughing.

"Your skin is so red right now."

"What are you doing?"

Miranda reached out for his hand.

"Can't we just enjoy the night getting to know each other without having to tell each other fake stories about other people?"

"I was hoping to hear about your idea of the perfect marriage," Douglas said.

"Okay, well, if we hit it off tonight, maybe that idea can come up more naturally. How about before we talk about that, though, we just talk about our interests? Or our hopes? Or anything that's normal for a first date?"

"A first date but not a last, right?"

Miranda held his gaze.

"Like I said earlier, how about we get through this one before we decide on whether there will be another?"

Douglas felt the small box in his pocket sticking to his hip. He hoped he hadn't just blown a lot of money he couldn't afford on a paperweight.

Chapter 4

WHEN THE SERVER BROUGHT the appetizers and took the main order, Douglas couldn't wait to dive in. As much as he wanted to keep talking about the future with Miranda, he didn't want to keep doing it with a brain that focused on an empty stomach. Feeding himself with warm food on a cold night was one way to get his mind back to a state of sensible thinking.

Their appetizers were nothing special, though. Even if they were dining out at a reasonably fancy place on the last night of the year, the food didn't match the occasion. No one was enjoying a plate of roasted snails or cooked vegetables with frosted tips or anything weird or interesting. Beyond the glass, everyone in view had something familiar on their plates. For Douglas and Miranda, they had mozzarella sticks and mild wings, four for each person.

Douglas dipped a mozzarella stick into a cup of marinara sauce and took a bite. Even as he savored the moment, Miranda did the same. This was the first time they'd eaten anything in front of each other since the impromptu lunch date last week that had started this whole dream.

It was also the perfect moment of silence to allow him time to think of a safer thread of conversation. So far, his choice to walk down Hypothetical Road hadn't yielded positive results.

Then again, she was still sitting here with him, either out of courtesy, or out of a genuine desire to see how the night went.

Whether she was curious if this would become a trainwreck, it was still too soon to tell.

"What did you want to be when you grew up?" Miranda asked when she finished her bite.

Douglas had just finished eating his own mozzarella stick when she'd asked the question. It was a question he hadn't thought about in years.

"Good question."

And it was a good question. What had he wanted to be when he grew up? He couldn't remember.

"Fireman," he said, when nothing better came to mind.

"How come you became a fertilizer salesman instead?"

Douglas shrugged. That was an easier question to answer, but not more exciting. Like most professionals in accidental professions, he'd just fallen into it. Sure, he'd hoped for a path that would satisfy his dreams, whatever they happened to be at the time, but that wasn't the path available to him.

"College degree funneled me into it," he said.

"Fire academy didn't work out then?"

He shook his head.

"I really don't remember what I wanted to be. Maybe it was a fireman. Could've been an astronaut. I just somehow ended up at college instead. This was the result."

Miranda nodded and smiled.

"I had a similar path," she said. "Not about the fake childhood dream, but definitely about the academic illusion."

"Yeah, what did you go in to do?"

Miranda thought about the question, then took another bite from her mozzarella stick.

"I'd originally wanted to be a psychologist."

"But now you market sales literature to companies?"

"Yep, that's the path of a woman who drops out of college before she gets her Masters."

"Did you get your Bachelors?"

She shook her head.

"Dropped out halfway through my junior year."

"Why?"

She sipped her water.

"Life has a funny sense of humor. In my case, it wasn't interested in sending me down that path any further."

"Again, why?"

"That sounds like a story for a later date."

Douglas studied her. He was no psychologist himself, but he could tell when someone was holding back important information, including information he'd probably want to know.

"I hope you'll tell it then."

The conversation drifted off toward other topics, including pet preferences and favorite love songs, the types of things that sometimes squeak through on a first date because when else would anyone bother to ask those types of questions? And in that volley of first-date essentials, the subject of hobbies came up. If they already knew what each other did for a living and how they each felt about their respective careers, both personally and in judgment of the other, then the topic of hobbies seemed like the logical follow-up.

"You first," Miranda said, when Douglas asked her the opening question.

She nursed her water while Douglas gave her his answer.

"I dabble in small things," he said, as he tried to figure out what his prime interests were. He enjoyed doing largely forgettable activities, like fixing his door handles whenever the screws came loose or walking down grocery store aisles more times than necessary whenever he wasn't yet ready to head home and just wanted to people-watch a little longer. But none of them were interesting date topics. Fortunately, he had one occasional activity he dabbled in that was likely worth talking about on a first date. "I also play the drums sometimes."

This perked Miranda up. She set her glass down and gave him her full attention.

"Oh, so you're a musician?"

"Sometimes."

"Have you ever played in a band?"

"Depends on your perspective."

Miranda wasn't sure how to digest that answer. Douglas wasn't surprised. It was intentionally vague.

"How about the perspective where you played in a band?"

Douglas reached for the last wing on the appetizer plate and dipped it in hot sauce. He'd already soaked up half the cup, and he was determined to finish it off with this last piece of chicken.

"I haven't technically played with other people live," he said. He ate a piece of his hot sauce-drenched chicken wing.

"So, you haven't played in a band?"

"Not in person, no."

Miranda shook her head.

"I don't understand your answer."

Douglas set the chicken bone down and licked his fingers clean. He wiped what remained of the hot sauce on his napkin.

"I play the drums in my living room. Usually, I perform solo, sometimes before I go to work. My neighbors don't really like it when I do that, though."

"You live in an apartment?"

"Exactly. But it's the only time I have the energy to practice. If I play in the evening, it's only for fun and relaxation. But I'm not learning anything from it."

"Do your neighbors have other instruments that they play through the walls first thing in the morning?"

Douglas laughed at the question. Miranda seemed pleased that he picked up on the joke.

"Not really the scenario I was painting, but I'd be lying if I said that never happened."

"What do they play?"

"The guy to my right has a saxophone. He usually bangs on my wall for me to stop, but he's occasionally joined in with my racket. I think he stops only when his neighbor bangs on his wall."

"Any of your neighbors have a guitar or piano?"

Douglas sipped his water to wash down the hot sauce.

"No. Most of my neighbors are boring. Just the saxophone guy, and he doesn't usually play."

"So, then what is your band by perspective?"

Douglas wasn't sure if his answer would land. More and more, he was beginning to see just how shallow his life was when he wasn't at work. There was no band. It was just the band he imagined playing with whenever he banged on those drums.

In his mind, he could picture himself on stage in some dingy nightclub with saxophone guy, and some pretend lead guitarist, a bassist, and a synth organ player. He could also picture a rail-thin rocker with tight spandex pants, an open shirt, tattoos all over his stomach, and lightning bolt earrings performing the vocals, as he inhaled whatever smoke permeated the room. Whenever the scene became complete in his head, he could then drum along whatever imaginary song he was thinking of, whether existing or one he'd craft on the spot.

To communicate this idea in as few words as possible, Douglas tapped the side of his head. Miranda nodded at him in response, as if she understood his "perspective."

"So, you're in an imaginary band?"

Douglas shrugged. When she said it that way, it seemed stupid, or even insane.

But it wasn't the incorrect way of saying it.

"So, really, you just play drums as a hobby."

"Well, yeah. That's basically what I said at the start."

Miranda drew her finger in circles on the table before her.

"You ever think about joining a real band?"

"Yeah, sure, I've thought about it. But I don't know anyone who plays."

"Your neighbor plays. What's his name?"

Douglas shrugged. "We've never spoken."

"You don't talk to your neighbors?"

"We never have a reason to."

"Even though you're neighbors?"

"Doesn't give us a reason to talk."

Miranda sipped her water. She was almost in need of a refill. So was Douglas.

"You should get to know your neighbors. Do you live alone? What if you have an emergency? Who's going to call the ambulance for you if no one knows you're in trouble?"

"Even if I did talk to my neighbors, I doubt they'd be in the room with me the moment that happened, not unless they're the ones causing the emergency."

"After all your early morning drumming?"

Douglas winked and pointed at her. Touché.

"What about you? What do you do for fun?"

Miranda couldn't delay the question this time. Douglas had already gone first. There was no one else to go second.

"Honestly," she said, "I don't have any hobbies."

"Of course you do. Everyone has something they enjoy doing."

Miranda tried to think of an answer, but nothing seemed to come to mind.

"Yeah, I don't really have anything. I don't watch much television or anything."

"You enjoy knitting?"

She gave him a weird look and chuckled.

"Why would I enjoy knitting?"

"I don't know. It's a thing to do."

She shook her head.

"I really don't have anything. I mean, when I was younger, I liked to swim a lot. I guess that was a hobby once upon a time."

"Why not now?"

"Well, it's winter, so I'm not going to do much swimming in winter. But honestly, I just don't have much time for hobbies."

"Too much time devoted to nursing school?"

"Among other things, yeah."

"They make you work long hours at the brochure place?"

"No longer than any other job would require. They aren't monsters there."

"So, how many hours of your week go to nursing school?"

"A few more than is probably healthy."

"But you're getting by?"

"I hope so. I'm taking my first series of exams soon."

Douglas swirled his water glass. Where was that server? They both needed refills soon.

"What would you do if you didn't have to put so much time in nursing school?"

"You mean, what would I do if I had time for hobbies?"

"Yeah."

Miranda thought about the question.

"I guess I would keep swimming in the summer. Maybe take up knitting in the winter."

Douglas pinched the bridge of his nose.

He could no longer tell if Miranda was taking the date seriously or just stringing him along until the night was over and she could get back to a stable life of brochures and nursing school without him.

Hopefully, she was just showing off her brilliant sense of humor.

At this point, her face wasn't quite giving away her secrets. Maybe she was messing with him. But maybe she was making fun of him.

Where was that server with their water refills?

The server checked in on them a few minutes later. When he saw how empty their glasses were getting, he snatched them, ran off, and resurfaced a minute later with freshly filled water glasses. Both Douglas and Miranda drank about half before the server walked away. Within moments, he came back with a third refill.

Not even a minute after the server left for the third time, a group of other waitstaff and host teams came swarming into the main dining room with a violinist in tow. The commotion was loud enough to register through the window.

"Uh-oh," Douglas said. "What's going on here?"

Miranda watched the show with him. The restaurant staff started a rhythmic clapping as they circled around a small table containing a younger couple, likely in their late twenties. Both the man and the woman were attractive, each one dressed in trendy clothes, and both were surprised by the restaurant staff closing in around them.

But the man's surprise faded away much faster than the woman's. Almost as soon as the violinist started in on a tune, the man seemed to understand what was happening. The woman was still clueless.

Douglas squinted as the staff got in so close to the table that the couple was barely visible. He could just see what was happening through the crack between two servers. Miranda, from her position, had a better view.

"I think I know," she said.

The man took the woman by the back of the hand and smiled at her. She looked nervous. The violinist's tune sounded a little like the theme to the birthday song, but it had a variance. Might've been the birthday song from another country, or one more thematic to the restaurant's brand. It was hard to tell through the staff's clapping and now Gregorian chanting.

As the staff's interference died down, the man said something to his date that made her smile. Her face was full of anticipation.

Miranda, meanwhile, made scoffing noises at them.

"This is so cheesy," she said.

"What is?"

"They're doing this on New Year's Eve in front of dozens of people. It's dumb."

"What's dumb?"

But Douglas didn't need to ask. He could see now what was happening. Something about the scene caused his stomach to lurch.

The man slipped out of his table and got down on one knee. The hand in his pocket slipped out with a small glittering object in hand.

Angela and Winston, who sat at the table next to them, were perplexed. Neither one had an animated reaction to the whole thing. Angela, in fact, looked bored by it. Winston looked confused. Other patrons at other tables appreciated the scene more. A few of them clapped as they recognized the event playing out before them.

"Seriously, why ruin that poor girl's life on New Year's Eve?" Miranda asked. "Couldn't you wait until Valentine's Day when it's dumber but more expected?"

Douglas had no comment. He felt frozen to his chair, unable to fully disagree with Miranda's assessment.

The usual buzz and fervor about the restaurant continued after the young couple returned to their seats, and the surrounding staff congratulated each other with handshakes and slaps on the back for orchestrating such a perfect engagement, after which they stalked off to their respective corners to continue the prosperous but ultimately performative job of satisfying the needs of strangers who would never bother thanking them if not for the requisite tip.

Douglas and Miranda also melted back into their positions as a couple on a first date, letting the vision and memory of the newly engaged couple slip out of view and out of mind.

Their main courses were still on order, so they had little else to do but stare at each other and attempt to hold a conversation that, in no way, implicated the pressures of a lifetime together as witnessing the pre-union of another couple might infer. Douglas thought the best thing to put Miranda's mind at ease was to ask her about her happiest memory.

She stirred her water with her straw as she considered her choices.

"Well, my happiest memory was ruined by my worst," she said, "so I'll have to tell you about my second happiest memory. Well, no, that one's too personal. Third? Also personal. My fourth was wonderful but also a bit—"

"Tell me about your tenth happiest memory," Douglas said. Clearly her happiest memories were topics for a more comfortable relationship.

"That's oddly specific." She started counting on her fingers as she considered whatever moments crossed her mind.

"Okay, maybe just tell me something you fondly remember."

She stopped counting and smiled at him.

"I remember going to the grocery store one evening and being surprised by a sale."

Douglas frowned. That wasn't a happy memory. In what world was that a happy memory? That was the type of incident that only Angela could find exciting.

"Tell me more," he said, doing his best not to grit his teeth.

She waved him off.

"No, that story isn't interesting. Just a fond memory. Well, except for the fact that I was broke due to other complications and didn't know how I was going to afford everything I needed that night."

Douglas gritted his teeth, but not at her story; at himself, for judging her too soon.

"Back in college, I take it?" he asked.

Miranda shrugged.

"A little more recent than that?"

Douglas leaned forward, hoping not to sound sarcastic, but also wanting to rule out scenarios that she didn't seem eager to share just yet.

"Was it yesterday?"

Miranda squeaked in laughter.

"No, I'm a bit better off today than I was back then, thankfully."

"But in the last ten years?"

She bobbed her head back and forth, somewhere between a yes and a no, but also ping-ponging in a way that suggested thought processes were nothing more than a tennis match.

"I think it's safe to admit this was in the last five years."

"But not yesterday?"

"Not yesterday."

Miranda held Douglas's gaze, daring him to dig deeper, to probe the uncomfortable question. But he was beginning to understand her pattern. Even if he asked, she was unlikely to tell him the truth, at least not all of it.

"You don't want me to know you very well, do you?" he asked, surprised by his own question. She was daring him, but he didn't expect to suddenly dare her. Maybe he was just tired of feeling jacked around tonight. He had fertilizer clients for that.

She reached out her hand and touched the back of his.

"Perhaps one day I'd like you to. But this is our first date. You're supposed to ask me what kind of ice cream flavors I like. It's a bit too soon to lay my life bare before you."

"I'll be bare before you if you'll be bare before me."

She squeezed his hand and looked away.

"That's not my style," she said. She released his hand. "Ask me about my favorite ice cream flavor."

"What's your favorite ice cream flavor?"

"Strawberry chocolate. What's yours?"

"Wasabi."

She smirked at him.

"What is it really?"

"Vanilla with peanut butter chips. I'm pretty simple."

She winked at him.

"And that's what I like about you."

<h1 style="text-align:center">Chapter 5</h1>

After a few minutes of casual ice-breaking conversation about topics that neither would remember talking about the next morning, their main courses arrived. The server seemed unnaturally pleased with himself for getting the food to the table in one piece. Douglas wondered if there was a point in the delivery at which they could not see him having a balancing issue that nearly ended in disaster. If so, the server was unlikely to ever admit it. Either way, he looked relieved when he set the plates down without breaking anything.

"Could I get you folks anything else?"

Douglas scanned the table. The appetizer plate had just one cheese stick and two wings left, plus a splatter of breaded crumbs that neither he nor Miranda was likely to scrape into a pile and eat. He was tempted to send the plate back with the server, but he also wasn't ready to admit that he was no longer interested in the appetizers now that his steak was here. How was he to know how hungry he'd be after eating his main meal? Maybe he wasn't eighteen anymore, but his appetite had not entirely abandoned him by his late thirties.

Likewise, his water was hovering at the midpoint between satisfactory and not full enough. Sure, it was usually a good idea to top off a beverage whenever the maximum opportunity for satisfaction was offered. But he also considered how inviting the server back so soon after sending him off would interfere with whatever conversation about dogs and cats he and Miranda were having.

"I think we're fine here," Douglas said.

"Actually," Miranda countered, "you could probably take the appetizers away. I don't think we're going to eat anymore."

Douglas almost objected, but he didn't want Miranda to think he was a hoarder. So, as the server thanked them for the opportunity to clear their table of a mostly empty plate, Douglas withheld his urge to lament the loss of his after-dinner cheese stick.

Once the server was gone, both Douglas and Miranda savored the moment studying their hot plates of meat and vegetables.

Douglas's steak was about two inches thick, squeezing juice out of every pore as the steam rose from its surface. The broccoli beside it glistened from the collateral moisture coming off the steak. Both appeared soft to the touch.

Miranda, meanwhile, leaned forward and breathed in the aroma of her chicken and vegetables, using her hand to fan in the scents. Like Douglas's meal, hers was a collection of softened meat made tender by the passing of time in a pressure cooker or some other heating preparation tool.

"This looks amazing," Miranda said.

Douglas couldn't help but agree. Yeah, they were just slabs of meat that anyone could get almost anywhere. But these were exceptional cuts, rarely duplicated by the lesser restaurants. They were also not as cheap.

"Okay, so let's dig in." Miranda was barely able to reach for her knife when her phone started ringing.

She glanced down at her open pocketbook, hesitant to answer. Even as she took her utensils in hand, she couldn't help but stare at the phone daring her to answer. By the third ring, she set down her fork and knife and gave in to temptation.

"Hello? Wait . . . slow down . . ." She held out the palm of her hand as if someone on the other line would see it. "Okay, calm down. This doesn't sound that bad." She glanced at Douglas, pleading with him to forgive her for this intrusion. Then she slipped out of her seat and stepped away from the table. "Okay, that doesn't sound good, either. All right start at the beginning. What happened?"

She stalked off past the neighboring table and headed to the railing by the pond to continue her unexpected conversation. Her voice became more garbled the farther she got away.

Douglas, meanwhile, was left alone, just him with his steak.

He wasn't sure if it was polite to eat without her, especially since the food was still hot. He took his fork and knife in hand and held each by the plate, each hovering close to the rim, each tempting him to dig into the meat and start cutting in.

He would give her three minutes to finish her call before he decided the meal was getting too cold to wait.

Less than a minute later, someone or something came shuffling up from behind him. The dull murmur of a woman's voice came with it.

"Well, look who it is," the strange female voice said off to his side.

He glanced over and immediately winced. His silverware slipped from his grip and clattered on the table.

Winston and Angela were each standing over him.

"What brings you here all by yourself on New Year's Eve?" Angela said, half condescending, half serious. "In the cold, no less."

Douglas rolled his eyes at their timing.

"I'm not here alone." He pointed at Miranda's plate. "I have a date."

Angela stared at the empty chair across the table.

"Of course you do. She's lovely."

"She's not here at the moment. She's taking a phone call. She's right over there."

He pointed at the spot by the lake where Miranda had stopped to talk to her caller. Only now, she wasn't there. In fact, she was nowhere he could see her.

"Oh, what a beauty," Angela said. "I can see why you like her so much. Does she quack?"

Douglas shook his head.

"I'm not alone."

"Sure you're not. So, when you and your 'date' finish here, why don't you come to the town clock and celebrate the New Year with us? That way you don't have to spend the stroke of midnight alone. I'd feel bad for you otherwise."

"I just said I'm not alone."

"Of course you aren't." Angela looked at the plate of chicken. "If you need help eating that, Winston here has quite the appetite."

"My date will be right back."

Angela winked at him. "But if she doesn't come right back, there's no shame in putting it in a box and eating it later. No one will judge you for it."

Douglas glanced at Winston, silently begging him for help. Winston, who still looked embarrassed to be there, simply waved, then looked for anywhere else he'd rather be, which, judging by the plant in the corner that had caught his attention, was anywhere.

"So, hope to see you at the clock soon," Angela said. She checked her phone. "Not much time left to go."

Angela grabbed Winston's arm and pulled him away from the table. Douglas wasn't sure from which angle they'd come from, as he didn't hear anyone coming through the door, and the patio had more than one way on and off, but they headed in a direction that likely opposed it, as if they were digital screensaver marbles that had just hit the edge of the screen and were now rebounding at a ninety-degree angle the other way. They were back inside and through the heart of the dining room and out of sight within seconds.

"Sorry about that," another voice said directly behind him. Miranda swooped in and took her seat. "The emergencies never stop. But everything's resolved."

She glanced at Douglas's steak. "Why aren't you eating? Your food is getting cold."

"I . . ."

Douglas had no answers. He barely understood what had just happened here.

Miranda, meanwhile, plunged her silverware into the chicken.

After the moment sharpened back into focus, Douglas recovered his own silverware from the table and dug into his steak. The juice seeped out from around both metal utensils and rode down the side of meat to the base of the plate. The beefy scent reached Douglas's nose and immediately caused him to forget the humiliating encounter he'd just endured.

Miranda took a bite of her chicken and closed her eyes as she savored it. Douglas did the same with his steak.

Now the date made sense. Man and woman, alone at a table, together, enjoying the beauty and luxury of two expensive but exquisite cuts of meat, together, as one, with no server or errant coworkers harassing them.

This was the moment Douglas had been waiting for. Not even their lunch at Olive Farm afforded them this divine moment of pleasure.

"Did I miss anything while I was gone?" Miranda asked.

Douglas swallowed his first bite.

"Not a thing," he said.

***

Douglas spent the remainder of dinner avoiding the question he wanted to ask about Miranda's phone call. At this point, he didn't see any reason to ask. She was unlikely to spill the details. If she expected tonight to have any magic, with him no less, she would keep all personal dramas to herself.

When both Douglas and Miranda finished the final bites of their food, the server materialized out of thin air to take their plates away, as if he'd been hovering over their tables in secret, or standing behind some secret pillar, just waiting for his moment to strike. The timing couldn't have been more tuned.

"Would you folks care for dessert this evening? We have the classics like peppermint apple pie, pumpkin tiramisu, and white chocolate peach cobbler, if I could interest you in any of them."

Douglas was already beyond his food intake limit and could feel his stomach looking for the escape hatch through his pants fastener. Miranda, who looked as if she was in less physical pain, considered the server's offer.

"Let's take a look."

She reached for the dessert menu and scanned its contents. Douglas, meanwhile, began the calculations in his head. How much had he already spent this evening?

- Steak and broccoli dinner. Expensive.
- Chicken and vegetable dinner. Expensive.
- Cheese stick and wings appetizer. Moderate.
- Two waters. Free.
- That special gift from the expensive store. Bank-breaking.
- Gas getting here. Expensive.
- Gas leaving here. Pending, but probably expensive.

Was there still room for dessert?

"Oh, the chocolate pie looks nice." She leaned toward Douglas with a smile. "Wanna share?"

"Of course."

Douglas's stomach was screaming at him to abort, but the opportunity to share a dessert with Miranda was one he didn't want to turn down.

"We'll share a slice," Douglas confirmed to the server.

The server bowed his head and scurried off to fulfill the order. Douglas took a sip of water to test whether he still had room for anything, much less a slice of pie. It hit bottom without incident.

While they waited, Douglas replayed the details from their conversation worth remembering, mostly of the various activities and foods Miranda had said she enjoyed. But he also took a mental note of her life goals, like graduating nursing school and becoming a nurse, as well as remembering what she did in her current busy time, selling books, booklets, and brochures to companies.

In his brief rewind of her life's story so far, however, he couldn't help but simmer on the reaction she had to his version of the perfect future with her or to her telling of the more nightmarish scenario with Winston and Angela. In both cases, she hinted that a happy life with another human being was impossible. But he wondered if she'd really thought that.

On the one hand, if she truly thought a long life with another human being could end only in tears, then it wouldn't have made sense that she'd come out tonight, not unless she was out only to get away from the realities of her hectic work and school life.

On the other hand, that break from busyness might've been the very reason she'd agreed to come out. Maybe she just wanted a night where she could spend time with another person that she wasn't trying to sell a brochure to or feed a dish of pills. Maybe she was neither a believer in a long-term relationship nor looking to start one. Maybe that was the reason for her many secrets tonight.

"You don't mind chocolate pie, do you?" Miranda asked suddenly. Had they been talking about something else? Douglas thought they were, but maybe the topic had been little more than noise. "I didn't stop to consider that you might've been interested in something else."

"No, chocolate is fine. Why do you think Angela would cheat on Winston in your version of their marriage?"

Now it was Miranda who was caught by surprise. She hesitated to speak, and when she was about to say something, she took another sip of her water and stared off toward the pond.

"Miranda?"

She shrugged and rolled her eyes.

"It's just a story," she said. "The odds that woman would marry that man or vice versa is pretty low by the look of the date they were having."

"Okay, but still. Why would you immediately go to the dark place?"

"Why would you immediately assume the happy place?"

Douglas wanted to say that he had no expectation of Winston and Angela ever becoming a permanent item, either, because why would they? But he had every expectation of himself and Miranda becoming a permanent item because that would make sense, and his happy marriage story was about them, not Winston and Angela. He wanted to tell her this. But he doubted she would understand.

"I think every marriage could be a happy one if you make it happy," he said.

She glanced back at him, this time with a semi-cold, semi-solemn expression on her face. She was about to give him bad news, but her sympathetic tone would take a backseat to a more realistic one, a less friendly one.

"Well, they can't," she said. "You're delusional if you think they can."

A moment later, the chocolate pie arrived with two forks on either side of it.

"Enjoy," the server said. Once his hand withdrew from the plate, he glanced at both faces, noticed the ice that had suddenly formed at the table, and backed away with little more than an inaudible apology.

Neither Douglas nor Miranda reached for a fork. They just stared at each other, caught somewhere between the next word and the next bite but inviting neither to be the first.

Meanwhile, the jewelry box in Douglas's pocket was getting heavier. If the sentiment didn't turn around soon, and quickly, his gift to her would become a gift to no one.

Maybe it was time he dropped the subject of a future with her.

Maybe he really was just dreaming.

But abandoning the topic didn't erase the question from his mind. She must've known someone who'd had a bad marriage once upon a time. It was the likeliest explanation for her response. It must've been so awful that she thought the idea inescapable that all marriages would have the same fate, as ridiculous as that was.

"What was your childhood like?" Douglas asked, changing the subject while also trying to root out the cause of her pessimism. His parents had never divorced, but he had friends whose parents had. He understood that plenty of families were broken by divorce and that many kids feared a similar fate for themselves someday. Perhaps Miranda was one of these children, or perhaps she had a best friend who—

Miranda reached for one of the forks and dug into the pie. Without a word, she took the first bite. Looked like she didn't want to answer that one, either.

***

Douglas had spent all week waiting for this night to come, and now that it was nearing its end, he wasn't confident about its success. From Miranda's late arrival to her dodged questions, to her mysterious phone call, to her icy shoulder given after his last serious question, the date seemed plagued with every bad omen that could befall a first run. If he weren't so dismayed by his bad luck, he would've found it all rather comical.

But he couldn't accept the evening as a comedy. After years of dipping in and out of relationships that had no momentum, if he could even call them relationships, watching one beauty after another exit his life without even a goodbye, he wanted one to work. Living alone had its perks, of course, and he certainly understood the value of freedom whenever he had the time to enjoy it. Late night action movies with no one but his neighbors to complain or leaving dishes to stack up in his sink for three days until he was inches away from inviting rats to live with him before deciding it was time to clean them up were activities he would've been saddened to sacrifice to the altar of woman-pleasing. But these freedoms were not worth the sacrifice of his happiness. He wanted a good woman to come home to, and Miranda had all the makings of a good woman.

She had composure, for one thing. Going back to school for a nursing degree in her thirties after missing out on education for so long was an act of bravery. Doing so while working the soulless, thankless job of selling brochures to companies that didn't want them demonstrated a measure of endurance. The best women could endure anything, especially the soulless and thankless things. Miranda was doing all of that.

And she understood his jokes. The last three women had the sense of humor of a wooden bat. The fourth-to-last woman laughed at everything, including his story about witnessing an old man falling off a park bench and cracking his ribs. Miranda had the right balance between good-humored and not-psychotic.

Of course, he couldn't forget her mesmerizing beauty. Her bright eyes captivated him whenever she wasn't looking elsewhere. And she understood how to apply the right amount of makeup—no clowns or Plain Janes here—just a woman who knew what makeup was made for. Even as she marched through her thirties, she had the structure that would survive the entrance to forty, even if she had to take on a few extra pounds on the journey. She had the form of a woman who could handle those few extra pounds and not look unhealthy.

Regardless of how he examined the angles, he couldn't find one that was a dealbreaker for him. Maybe she was having a bad time and was struggling to maintain her grace tonight, but she was still holding on to her grace. Even if she'd grown to hate him in the last two hours, she was doing a masterful job not throwing the disdain in his face. She seemed like the type of woman who would withhold her curses for him until after she got into her car and drove off.

Douglas was unlikely to ever meet a better woman than Miranda.

So, he had to salvage the moment in whatever way he possibly could. But given his track record with women and bad dates, he wasn't sure how.

Miranda, meanwhile, picked at the chocolate pie, half interested in its offering. She scraped the prongs across the rich surface, drawing four-lane tracks from tip to crust. And when she finally reached a point where she could drag the fork no further, she brought it to her mouth and licked the chocolate off the edges. Then she'd stare at the pie, decide whether to take another bite, or scrape the fork across the surface in the other direction. In any case, she was less interested in the pie than she was when she first ordered it.

"Would you like me to help you eat that?" Douglas asked, somewhere between helpfulness and fearful of wasting money on an uneaten piece of dessert.

Miranda shrugged.

"There are two forks. May as well."

Douglas dug his fork along the left edge and shaved off some chocolate. For a slice that cost the price of a whole pie anywhere else, it tasted remarkably like regular, unremarkable chocolate pudding. Perhaps the value was in the texture. It certainly held together competently.

"Not bad," he said.

Miranda took another bite for herself. She looked pleased but not ecstatic about the taste. Her expression said, *Well, that's certainly a slice of chocolate pie*, maybe not disappointed by the experience of eating it, but not fanning herself from overstimulation by it, either. Each new bite had less enthusiasm than the one before. Douglas couldn't help but wonder if she'd enjoy it more if he hadn't cast the dark shadow of an imposing question on her first.

He wanted to say something that would make her laugh, completely change the mood back to something light and fun. But he was out of ideas. Every word felt like the next step through a minefield, and he was tired of marking the next danger zone.

So, he said nothing. Just plunged his fork into the pie and took another bite.

Miranda did the same.

And somehow, when they went in for the next bite, they'd missed their rhythm. Both attacked the same spot at the same time, interlocking their forks together. Pulling them apart took a level of coordination that neither could summon immediately, but they tried. With the force of metal tugging against metal and the gel of chocolate pie keeping them fused together, the act of separating their forks became its own farcical event. It was a stupid thing, but it was ridiculous enough to make them both chuckle at it.

"I think we're overcomplicating this," Miranda said. She jiggled her fork sideways, attempting to free it from the pie and the grip of Douglas's own fork. "This is hardly a Chinese finger puzzle."

"Or maybe our forks are just demonstrating the action we should be taking for ourselves."

Miranda laughed at that one.

"And you say I have a dirty mind."

Douglas realized the suggestion he'd just made and felt his cheeks flush.

"No, I was just making a point that—"

Miranda touched the back of his hand.

"Don't apologize. It's funny."

She held his gaze for just a moment before returning her attention back to her pie. But it was a moment that lasted long enough. The ice had thawed again, his last stupid question now forgotten. The tension in her cheeks relaxed.

When Miranda managed to free her fork from his, she seemed to enjoy the next bite a little more. Douglas did, too.

Chapter 6

D OUGLAS SPENT THE LAST few minutes of dessert speaking as little as possible, leaving the dead air open to Miranda to fill in with her own topics of discussion. Because they were just moments from getting the bill and the subtle suggestion from the server to get the hell out so he can make new money off the next party, Douglas knew whatever she talked about would be anodyne but short-lived, and sure enough, the words out of her mouth compared the chocolate pie to something she ate earlier in the week. He nodded as if he cared, and maybe he did a little, but he was mainly just happy that she was talking at all.

When the hefty bill finally arrived, Douglas allowed the sharp pain in his stomach to run its course, then handed his credit card off to the server. While waiting for the payment to process, Miranda excused herself, leaving Douglas alone with his thoughts.

Was the price of a dinner with Miranda at a cost of nearly a full day's salary worth it? If Miranda were his dream partner, then he would say yes. And she was definitely his dream partner. But the value magnified on the condition that she agreed to see him again. So, the real question was whether this dinner was worth the cost of the next one. For that, he'd wished Miranda had opened up to him more.

He couldn't help but wonder whether she would still be his dream partner if he knew the answers to the questions she refused to answer.

The server returned with the credit card copy for Douglas to sign. Douglas added a twenty-five percent tip to his already overpriced bill. He didn't offer high gratuity to the man for being an exceptional deliveryman of hot food, but rather because the server had the good sense to leave him mostly alone to enjoy his date in peace. He'd had previous dates ruined by overzealous servers who couldn't stand being out of the conversation or avoid being opinionated on how his date was dressed. In fairness, his past dates were often at sketchier restaurants that doubled as truck stops and featured breakfast items for dinner. Perhaps this server's lack of intrusion was factored in the price of the bill.

Once the server closed out the ticket, Miranda still hadn't returned, so Douglas visited the restroom to wash his hands and check his face. His hair was still neat and in place, but his skin was red in patches. He wasn't allergic to anything on the menu, so he was likely just looking at his reaction to stress. His face often broke out like this after an important deal with a farmer.

The night out with Miranda was a big deal, but he supposed future dates would cause him less tension. At some point, the two of them would be comfortable with each other, and a night at some fancy restaurant would no longer serve as some classic invitation for the jitters but a thing they did to stay connected. He looked forward to that point in their future long history where that comfort would slip right into place.

When he returned to the table, she was still missing, so he searched the restaurant for a hidden corner where she might've been on the phone. When he couldn't find her anywhere inside, he checked out the front door. He finally found her standing along the sidewalk, her arms folded over her chest, and her eyes staring off into the distance.

"We're all set," Douglas said, when he approached her. She glanced at him and smiled. "What are we in the mood for now?"

Miranda wiped her hands down her long sleeves and extended her right hand for a shake.

"This was fun," she said. "Thanks for the distraction. I should probably get going, though."

Douglas almost reached for her hand, his stomach suddenly falling into his pelvis. But he stopped himself. The night was still early, mostly. Plenty of time for more of the date to happen.

He refused to part ways just yet, not without hearing a good reason for it, especially since he still had that expensive gift to give her. This was hardly the time or place to hand something so special, and so credit-killing, off to her. His plan was to present it to her at midnight when it would be at its most memorable.

"Could I interest you in a walk first? We could burn off a few calories in the meantime. Just a few though. That pie was pretty rich."

Miranda tossed the idea around in her mind. She checked her phone, perhaps for the time, perhaps for an excuse to escape, but nothing she saw seemed to concern her too much. So, she shrugged.

"Yeah, all right."

Douglas had no destination in mind, as the countdown to midnight at the downtown clock was not for another couple of hours, and heading there now would just push them into a gathering crowd of gawking strangers sooner than he would like. Not to mention, he risked running into Winston and Angela long before he was ready to see either of them again. So, he just started walking and let the whims of random directions at various intersections determine where they might end up.

That level of chance brought them to a corner park by an ornamental fountain decorated in holiday lights. They each took a moment to appreciate the soft beauty it brought to the neighboring businesses in the area around it.

While they watched the icy water spit four feet above the basin and fall in chunky water drops and mist, Douglas dared to reach for her hand, not to shake it, but simply to hold it. Miranda accepted it for just a moment, then released it. She said nothing in response. She just watched the water.

"You know," Douglas said, his thoughts replaying the entirety of their dinner on fast-forward, "to answer your earlier question about the perfect marriage, I do have a reasonable answer for you, if you want to hear it."

"Not really. The topic is meaningless."

"Humor me?"

"Does it involve your two work friends?" She was looking at him now. "Because I don't want to hear anything more about them. They depress me."

Douglas chuckled at that remark. They depressed him, too.

"No, I can make it about us, about our possible future, if you agree to see me again."

Miranda considered the offer.

"We just met. It's too soon for all these hypotheticals." Even as she spoke the words, she held his gaze. Her eyes were too soft this time to signal a warning. Perhaps she was going more for caution.

"It's just storytelling," Douglas said. "Doesn't have to mean anything."

"But we both know it'll mean something to you."

Douglas shrugged. "Why do you say that?"

"Because you won't drop the topic."

"I promise it'll be a good one this time."

Miranda said nothing.

"Please?" Douglas said. "I think you'll like this one."

She folded her arms over her chest.

"I'm skeptical. But maybe also a little curious." She nodded. "Yeah, all right. Let's hear it."

Douglas smiled at her. He had to make this one count. Any future happiness he'd hoped to share with her depended on him not screwing this one up.

He needed to give her some hope that he was worth her time. Maybe then his gift wouldn't seem like such a waste of mega money, or such a lunatic thing to give on a first date when he inevitably passed it off to her.

He took a deep breath.

Then he uttered the words of hopefulness that were laced with such utter fearfulness.

Hopeful New Wife

REGARDLESS OF WHATEVER DISTURBING or debaucherous things Winston and Angela were doing to each other in the bakery at the supermarket, Douglas would not concern himself with them. He was here to find Miranda the perfect cheesecake, preferably one with raspberries. Based on conversations they'd had in the past, he'd concluded that this was her favorite, and therefore the perfect treat for her 29th birthday, here in November . . .

The perfect treat for her 34th birthday here in April, on the 16th—on the 17th, a day he would never forget.

Yes, on her 34th birthday on April 17th, the loveliest day of the year, Douglas would bring Miranda home the sweetest, cheesiest cheesecake she had ever seen or tasted, full of cheese and raspberry and—

Or rather, he would bring her the chocolate turtle cheesecake because that was her actual favorite, even though she did like the raspberry flavor.

When Douglas snatched the chocolate turtle cheesecake out of the hands of a greedy deadbeat who most definitely didn't need it, he ran for the checkout counter before he could get the dessert wrong. Miranda would get much chocolate tonight, and no slob with chocolate-covered sweat stains would prevent her from her birthday bliss.

Douglas didn't wait for the receipt. He made a dash for the car before anyone could demand retribution against his swift thinking and wreck his plans.

Because Miranda was worth it, Douglas also stopped by a flower shop on the way home. The shop offered plenty of choices among her favorites from tulips to roses to . . . the naked man orchid? The hell?

Yes, even the naked man orchid, Miranda's all-time favorite. That purple Mediterranean native with two arms and three legs would come home with Douglas and go right into Miranda's favorite planter.

Because she was worth it.

Once again, Douglas got into his car with Miranda's latest gift, when, wouldn't he know it, a jewelry shop beckoned him to stop and look inside.

And again, the choices he had at his disposal . . . yes, were too expensive, and far too extravagant for any occasion, and why would he stop at such a place and blow his budget and his salary on a birthday gift? How irresponsible!

But there was a nice affordable necklace made from fool's gold that still sparkled under the fluorescent lights and would've looked perfectly reasonable around her neck. And because Miranda had no qualms about him spending less than a hundred dollars on gifts for her birthday, he had no qualms about the twenty dollars it cost him to get that fake gold necklace wrapped up and put in a very inexpensive box.

After he thanked the jeweler for making Douglas's new wife's birthday the best one she's ever had, or will have, as the day was still young and she had yet to receive her gifts, he once again returned to his car, considered his inventory, checked that the cheesecake hadn't melted in the springtime sun, and headed in the direction of home, keeping his attention fixed to the road for as long as possible to avoid any temptation to spend even more money on the woman who was worth spending all the money in the world.

Of course, he passed his favorite pizza place on the way home, and Miranda loved pizza . . . yes, she loved pizza, so he ordered a pie. Pepperoni, sausage, er, pineapple . . . seriously?

He ordered a pepperoni, sausage, and pineapple pizza with—no, just pepperoni and sausage. The pineapple was just a joke. Douglas ordered—never mind. He bought more stuff that made Miranda happy and came home with it all. He assumed everything he picked up was something she would like.

As he entered the hallway leading to his apartment, his landlady, Miss Nancy, stepped out of her front door and squinted at the boxes in his hand.

"That why you're always late on rent?" she asked.

Douglas tried moving past her, but she zipped in his way. He was surprised at how quick and limber a woman her age could get whenever rent was involved.

"Where you going?" she demanded. "Why the hurry?"

Douglas nodded at his front door a few feet down the hall.

"My wife's birthday. Have to celebrate."

Miss Nancy's composure changed. Her demanding expression turned to delight.

"Oh, how wonderful. That Miranda is such a fine woman." She narrowed her gaze at him. "Though, I have no idea what she sees in you."

Douglas nudged forward.

"Do you mind? The cheesecake is melting, and the pizza is getting cold?"

Miss Nancy studied his stack of boxes and plastic bags. Whether she noticed his precarious balancing act before, she acknowledged it now.

"Very well. Because I wouldn't want to ruin your lovely wife's birthday, I will allow you to pass this time. But I want my rent. Tomorrow. No more delays."

"Isn't rent due at the beginning of the month?"

Miss Nancy was about to speak, but then she mouthed some numbers as she considered the items in her mind. She appeared to be counting something. Maybe the days since Douglas's last payment on the first of the month. Once she reached her conclusion, her face softened, and she smiled at him.

"Ah, you're right. You are caught up, aren't you?" Her face narrowed again. "You're late so much I can never keep up anymore."

Douglas took another step towards the door. "Mind if I go home now?"

The landlady stepped aside and ushered him past.

"Yes, yes, don't keep your lovely wife waiting. Wish her a happy birthday for me, if you don't mind."

"Sure."

Douglas continued past her. If Miss Nancy wanted to wish Miranda a happy birthday, she could do it on her own time. He didn't owe that woman anything—

Except, Miranda would've appreciated any message from neighbors wishing her a happy birthday, even the usually nasty ones who always demand money, so he made a point to pass the message along anyway, because this was her day, not his. His personal feelings didn't have to interfere with Miranda's happiness.

When Douglas entered the apartment, he found the living room empty, so he took his moment of solitude to search for the best place to hide her gifts. Even though today was her birthday, he didn't want to just spring everything on her. Layering the evening with a new gift to discover each hour was the better way to go. He started by putting the pizza on the counter. It was dinnertime, after all. No point in hiding that one.

The refrigerator was the obvious place to store the cheesecake, as he didn't want it to get watery. But setting it on the center shelf at eye level was the wrong place for it. Instead, he carved out a comfortable nook behind the ketchup and barbecue sauce. Even if Miranda got a craving for milk or celery, she was unlikely to look behind the barbecue sauce for either—not that she needed any celery because she was already the perfect shape and had no need to drop another pound through guilt eating, of course.

Once the cheesecake was stowed out of sight, Douglas searched for the ideal place to hide the naked man orchid. He worked in fertilizer sales by trade, so he knew something about soil, but he knew very little about individual flowers that he'd never heard of. The basics, like roses and dandelions, he could make do, but the advanced orchid variants were another beast he never knew how to tame, so he didn't know whether it needed a lamp or a damp closet to survive the night. For now, he compromised by putting it under the nightstand in the corner of the living room where the lamplight bled a little into the dark alcove and the upstairs apartment bathroom occasionally leaked down his wall.

Hiding the necklace was another kind of challenge, however. There were plenty of places he could put it where Miranda would never find it. But he worried those same places would be so obscure that he would also forget how to find it. So, he needed someplace that, in a pinch, Miranda would stumble upon it, even if she did not do so tonight. The only place he could think of was under the kitchen sink, draped over the neck of one of the cleaning bottles. At some point, she would look under there.

Now that all her gifts were sufficiently hidden, Douglas searched for her whereabouts. He knew she was home because he could hear her making noises, like squeals or little cries, in one of the backrooms. She was likely in bed watching funny videos on her phone, but she could've just as easily been reading a book. Either way, he checked for her in the most likely place at the start.

When he found her in the bedroom, she wasn't watching videos or reading books. She was scurrying on the bed, avoiding a rat that had made residence on the floor.

The rat was small, barely of adult size, and colored in the mangiest gray he'd seen in weeks. It sat at the foot of the bed, staring up at the base of the mattress, daring itself to jump. The woman standing at the far end, over the pillows, could not see the creature herself, as the foot of the bed obscured her view. But she nudged her attention to both sides, attempting to see if the rat had moved to a higher position on the floor.

"Never fear," Douglas said, as he assessed the situation and considered his skill at rodent stomping, "I'm home now. I'll take care of this."

He found some roach spray in the corner of the room and uncapped it. Whether the poison was strong enough to kill a rat, he didn't know, but he was ready to find out. Miranda, meanwhile, begged him not to spray it.

"I don't want it killed," she said. "I just want it out of here."

Douglas set the spray down. He didn't yet have experience at escorting mangy rodents out of the apartment, so he didn't have a plan.

But he was resourceful, and he would use his skills of resourcefulness to please his wife any way he could, even if it meant trying all the methods he could think of, from whistling for the rat's attention, to fanning it with books, to—

Okay, he found an empty plastic bin in the closet and dropped it over the rat. It didn't really need so much over-thinking. Once he slid a sheet of cardboard under the bin's opening, he could flip the bin over, trapping the rat in the basin. From there, it was a matter of taking the rat outside and dumping it in the park across the street.

When he returned to the apartment, Miranda was in the kitchen, serving herself a slice of pizza onto their finest ceramic plate.

"I assume this is dinner," she said.

"For my birthday girl," Douglas said.

He resisted the urge to kiss her. Pizza and lips didn't always go well in combination, especially when the pizza already had pepperoni on top.

Once they finished eating their respective slices at the dinner table, Douglas excused himself and headed for the refrigerator. He didn't explain why he was looking for more food. He just went in and produced the cheesecake.

"Ta-da," he said, as he stood the ketchup and barbecue sauce bottles he'd knocked over when he retrieved the dessert. "Your favorite."

Miranda insisted she had no room for dessert, but she thanked him for thinking of her. When Douglas cut a slice out for himself, Miranda relented.

"I'll just take a bite of yours," she said.

Douglas was perfectly happy sharing his slice with her, even though she had seven-eighths of the rest of the pie remaining that she could get for herself. What was his was hers.

Over the course of the hour, Douglas revealed the other gifts, beginning with the orchid and ending with the necklace. Miranda found a spot over the bed to hang the orchid and a spot on the dresser for the necklace. She promised to wear the necklace the next time they went out on a dinner date. Douglas invited her to wear it around the apartment, too, if she wanted, but she insisted that that would've been weird. Douglas said he agreed.

Finally, as the night wound down and they watched a movie about a billionaire seducing a secretary into a happier life of BDSM, Miranda was getting sleepy, so they ended the movie early and got ready for bed. Miranda was feeling a little tense around the shoulders, so she stood under a hot shower to ease the tension. Because he wanted her to feel better, Douglas got into the shower with her and massaged her shoulders. She melted under his touch. It was the relaxation she needed.

Once they were out and dressed, Douglas in his knee-length shorts and Miranda in her very conservative pink pajamas, they headed off to bed, where no pillows were too hard on the neck and no rats were waiting to jump in with them.

While in bed, Miranda read a chapter of her latest paperback under the soft light of the bedside reading lamp. This light did not bother Douglas in the slightest. If he needed to sleep in darkness, he could just put a pillow over his face. He was more interested in keeping Miranda happy.

Once she finally put the book down and turned off the light, she leaned over to Douglas, kissed him on the cheek, and thanked him for the lovely birthday. Then, as she lay back on her side of the bed and relaxed her head onto her softest pillow, she closed her eyes and smiled. At that point, the neighbors' bed started thumping hard against the wall, and one of them began screaming. Miranda reached out and took Douglas by the hand. Douglas didn't own a fan before or during their marriage, so the neighbors' thumping was their white noise. Now that the noise had started and the opposite neighbors started yelling at them to keep it down, Douglas and Miranda could fall asleep together.

Douglas and Miranda had been wandering throughout downtown during his story, peering into flower shops that had closed for the evening, late-night pastry shops that would have been perfect to visit had they not already gorged on chocolate pie, and a pet store where the puppies stared at them with their doughy eyes, pleading for escape—all the usual places a successful date on the verge of romance would encounter if the travel plan were more deliberate, places where Douglas couldn't be sure his subconscious hadn't already pre-arranged.

But now, at his story's conclusion, they were standing alongside a railing overlooking a frozen creek by the roadside. It might've just been a runoff ditch. But regardless, they were within sight of the clock downtown and the crowd of hundreds gathering around it.

Miranda was staring across the ice at the lights in the distance. She was thinking about something. Maybe the story. Maybe the date. Whatever it was, she was lost in it.

When she finally spoke, she let out a soft sigh.

"I must admit," she said, "that does sound rather nice."

Douglas smiled at himself. Miranda didn't see him.

"But I have a hard time believing it," she continued. "It's too nice."

Douglas's smile faded. Maybe it was the late December temperatures at work, but he could not understand why Miranda's heart was so frozen tonight.

"It's realistic," he said.

Miranda's face was kind, but she had no interest in entertaining him or his feelings.

"It's not, though. Plus, you left out a few key details. For example, I have a house. Why would we live in a small apartment with landladies and loud neighbors? Nothing about it is realistic. I doubt you'd be so nice in reality, not after the honeymoon ends."

Douglas considered the relationships of people he knew throughout life: his parents, his friends, his classmates. Most of them didn't have perfect relationships with their spouses or partners, but they did have functional relationships, certainly the kind that would've fit comfortably in his idea of the not-so-perfect-but-good-enough marriage. If Miranda thought that was unrealistic, it was possible then that she thought marriage itself was unrealistic.

"What do you consider the ideal marriage then?" Douglas asked.

She thought about the question, then shrugged.

"I don't," she said.

Even as she said it, the lights in the distance sparkled in her eyes. Maybe it was a trick. Maybe it was just Douglas's optimism toying with his vision. But even in her pessimism, he saw beauty in her. She was murdering his dreams to his face, and yet she had the softness of a pillow in her eyes. She wanted to be truthful without hurting his feelings. It was a dichotomy that didn't work, but he found her beautiful for trying.

"Then what's the ideal date?" he asked.

She shrugged again.

"I don't know." She thought about the question as she watched the sparkling lights across the ice. "This has been kind of nice, though. Not perfect." She looked at him square in the eyes. "Maybe I shouldn't admit that, though."

Douglas reached for her cheek. She flinched.

"You should. And you did."

She backed away. Her attention went immediately past his shoulder. She nodded in the direction of the clock.

"We should head over there now if we want a good spot for the countdown."

Miranda moved past him before he could say another word.

Chapter 7

IN THE COURTYARD BY the clock, Douglas and Miranda found a small space carved out of the crowd near a bench and a trash can that had already reached maximum density. When they got in range, they understood why no one wanted to stand near it. It was rotten.

"We could move into the field," Douglas said, when they agreed this was the worst spot. "At least we'll have more room."

"I don't want to stand in the snow," Miranda said. However, once she glanced at the overflowing trash can, her face looked conflicted.

In the back of his mind, Douglas agreed with her. Standing in the snow was not ideal. But nothing about sharing a courtyard with half the town in the year's final hour was appealing. The only reason Douglas came out tonight was because Miranda came out here with him. Otherwise, he'd be home sitting on his couch, wrapped in a blanket and watching old 1980s action movies. Because of her, standing in the cold with half the town, smelling whatever was left of fifty unfinished lunches was acceptable. If moving into the field eliminated the more negative variable, he would tolerate it.

"I'll take off my jacket and let you stand on it," he said.

Miranda smirked at him. Once again, she got the joke. If anyone was ever a keeper, Douglas decided she was it.

"Maybe we should keep looking for a spot closer to the clock," she said.

Douglas shrugged. He was already here. It didn't matter to him where they stood, as long as they reached midnight there together.

They pushed through the crowds, inching little by little toward the center where the clock stood, casting its show of time across the heads of all who attended tonight. Several times, they reached a fissure between groups that looked promising but proved fruitless when those same groups closed in around them, nearly splitting Douglas and Miranda apart. By the third unsuccessful attempt and near loss of each other, Douglas reached out for Miranda's hand and held on for the rest of the journey.

But somehow, they kept getting closer to the clock. And closer. And closer.

And then—

"Oh, look who it is," the familiar voice of the woman he didn't want to see again until her vacation ended next Monday said. "See, Winston, I told you he'd come looking for us."

Douglas couldn't see either of his workmates, but he could feel their presence just a few feet away, perhaps from behind another pair of strangers. Angela's dirty blonde hair was just within sight through the narrow crack between an older man and his wife or girlfriend, though most of it was hiding under her white wool cap, which loomed over the older man's head. Winston's wild dark mane was easier to spot, since it always reminded Douglas of a tired rock star who had fallen out of bed at four in the afternoon.

"Hey Douglas, wanna join—" Angela had trouble getting his attention, though he could hear her without issue. She kept darting her head from side to side, trying to catch a glimpse of him from between the older couple's shoulders.

Douglas pulled Miranda along, trying to get farther away. But Miranda resisted.

"I think some people are trying to talk to you," she said.

"Hey Douglas," Angela said again. "Can you see us?"

Douglas stopped moving, stuck between a family of four and a family of six. Even if he wanted to keep going, these human obstacles created a wall he could not route through. He'd have to go around, likely right through Winston and Angela.

He sighed.

"Yeah," he said. "I can see you."

"Great." Angela shoved her hands between the older man and his date and ignored their protest as she cast them aside. "Since you're alone, you should join—"

She spotted his hand intertwined with Miranda's hand, and her eyes widened at the sight of it. She glanced up to look at Miranda. Recognition flashed in her face almost immediately.

"Hey, aren't you the woman with the sales brochures?" she asked.

Miranda rolled her eyes. Without missing a beat, she moved past Douglas and pulled him along with her. Wherever they were spending the stroke of midnight, it would not be here, and not in earshot of the woman who had disrespected her business and wasted her time on Christmas Eve when it became clear she was never interested in the product she was selling.

Granted, they couldn't get too far away. The crowd was so thick that mobility required strategy, and the late hour was eating into their ability to plan the next move. At some point, they would have to stop. And as the clock entered its final half-hour, they decided they'd moved far enough. Wherever they were standing now, this was where they would spend their Happy New Year.

Miranda would spend it squeezed in between Douglas and some dude who must've lifted weights for a living. Douglas would spend it standing on a discarded half-eaten cartoon of noodles.

It was at that point Miranda let go. Now that they were no longer moving, there was no need to stay tethered. No one in the crowd would split them up, not without force or intention.

And now that the adrenaline had wound down, they had nothing else to say.

A minute passed when Douglas felt the weight of their silence pressing against the backdrop of everyone else's loud chatter. Miranda kept her attention on the clock as she fidgeted in place, likely wishing midnight would hurry so she could get out of here. Douglas felt that urge to escape himself. He didn't enjoy standing deep in the heart of any large crowd, even when the woman of his dreams stood with him. Finishing the conversation would've broken that discomfort.

But he wasn't sure what else to talk about. So many topics bandied around them that he could no longer think of one for himself. So, he said nothing. He just stood there with her.

The best form of communication he could summon amid the clatter of empty voices and disjointed words and phrases around them was to once again reach for her hand. He figured they'd already held hands several times tonight. What was another during their moment of stillness?

Douglas reached out and took her hand, half expecting her to slap it away. Maybe he shouldn't have expected it, since the point of a date was to breach the awkwardness between strangers and form a connection that might bond them. But he did. Thanks to their rocky start on Christmas Eve and Miranda's tenuous ability to trust him with information, he couldn't tell if he was winning or losing the night with her.

To his relief, however, she didn't pull away. She'd kept her hand still, almost limp, and at first, he wondered if it had frozen numb and she couldn't feel her knuckles resting in his palm. But when she looked at him, then glanced at her hand and shrugged, he had no doubt that she intended to stay put. Perhaps she still couldn't feel his hand against hers. Her knuckles were cold, almost icy. But then, maybe that was her reason for keeping his grip. Maybe he was warming her up.

Without warning, Miranda leaned in close.

"I owe you an apology," she whispered in his ear. Her breath was welcome heat in the cold air.

"What for?" he whispered back.

"Your story was very nice. But I can't buy it."

Douglas wanted to be surprised by her admission, but he wasn't. A part of him didn't buy it, either. No marriage was flawless.

"Why not?"

"Because I believed in it once upon a time."

Douglas shrugged. Didn't all little girls believe in it once up on a time, just to get jaded in adulthood after witnessing friends and family screw it up? For that matter, didn't the boys get jaded, too?

"Not all fairy tales have to come true," Douglas said. "They just have to inspire hope."

"But that hope only lasts until it's shattered by reality."

Douglas reached for her chin and turned her toward him so he could look her in the eyes.

"Why the cynicism? Just because others have bad experiences doesn't mean you will. You can't know for sure until you've experienced it for yourself."

Miranda said nothing. She just stared at him, stone-faced.

It took maybe five seconds for Douglas to finally under-stand what she'd been hiding from him all night. Her silence filled him in on the missing piece.

"Oh. I get it now."

Miranda said nothing.

"You were married once upon a time," he said, not a question, but a probe for confirmation.

Miranda offered him a shallow smile.

"What happened?" he asked.

"How does it always happen?"

"I don't know. I've never been married."

"And that explains your optimism."

Douglas almost felt the punch to his gut, but he steeled himself up against it. His pulse was picking up speed in his neck. Miranda had been keeping this secret from him all night for reasons unknown. But he was keeping one from her.

Now was as good of a time as any to share it.

"No, I like you. My desire to make you happy explains my optimism."

Miranda was about to respond, but she stopped herself. Perhaps she had nothing to respond to.

Instead of retorting or shooting him down, she simply turned back toward the clock and leaned the side of her head against his chest. Douglas couldn't help but notice that she was still holding his hand.

It took maybe a minute for her to finally speak.

"The problem is you may not always like me. Not enough."

"Well, I don't like myself most of the time, but I still live with myself. Not planning to change that any time soon."

Miranda glanced up at him. He could feel her breath on his cheek. Maybe he was finally piquing her curiosity.

But she said nothing more.

Midnight was coming.

Nothing more to do but wait for its arrival.

Well, maybe there was still one thing he could do in these last seven minutes.

Chapter 8

EVERYTHING ABOUT TONIGHT SEEMED like it was offering itself up to chance. They were supposed to meet on Saturday, but some emergency had prevented it, leaving them instead with New Year's Eve as their option. Then, despite every effort to have a good time tonight, the mood kept crashing, rising and falling. One moment they're smiling, another they're sidestepping offense.

The night was an ocean wave, and like the tide that goes back out to sea, they had no guarantee of a repeat for better or for worse. And because Douglas didn't know if he'd ever see her again once the clock struck midnight and they went their separate ways, he decided he had nothing left to lose but the huge chunk of change he'd possibly wasted on the gift she likely didn't want.

As anticipation for the New Year stirred in the crowd louder, harder, faster, Douglas released her hand and reached in his coat pocket for the small box from Ritzy and Respectable.

There was no room in this packed crowd to make any sort of grand gesture. He could hardly move far enough to stand before her. They were so pressed into each other that reaching into his pocket was difficult. To remove the box was even harder. It required him to bend his elbow into occupied space. But it also required him to slide his hand along Miranda's side, as the box was in the pocket pressed against her thigh. There was no way she wouldn't notice what he was doing.

As Douglas slid his hand out of his coat pocket, Miranda jutted her hip sideways to give him enough room to move.

They looked down at the box in his hand together.

"What's that?" she said, her voice a bit strained.

"A token of my faith that you're worth my time and future," he said.

She drifted a few inches away. The chill of the night found the crack between them and seeped in.

"I sure hope you're just planning to show me something pretty and have no other intention."

Douglas opened the box, careful not to drop it. If it hit the ground, it was gone. The crowd was too dense to give him room to bend down or find it again.

He angled it so she could see it clearly. Inside was the diamond ring that Astrid the jeweler had talked him into buying, perhaps foolishly, but maybe wisely.

"What do you think?" he asked.

"It's shiny."

She was right. Even in the dull glow of the courtyard's ambient lighting, the diamond glittered.

"Wanna wear it?"

Miranda's shoulders sank. If she wanted to avoid the question and run away, she was out of luck. She was stuck here with him; no choice but to consider the offer.

"It's way too soon to—"

"Yeah, you keep saying that. All you gotta do is put it on. You don't need to commit to anything. But I already know what I want. I didn't make a fool of myself last week because I was testing the waters. I didn't ask you here tonight because I was testing the waters. I don't need testing. I made my decision on Christmas Eve. Whatever happened before with that other guy, it won't happen again with me."

"You don't know that—"

"I do know that."

"How?"

Douglas closed the box and handed it to her. She could decide when to put the ring on her finger. For now, he would just entrust her to hold on to it until she was ready to keep it or sell it.

"I used to think love at first sight was a joke. I still do. But now I understand why people claim to 'just know.' That's what I discovered last week when you walked into our office. You standing there at the reception desk, exploring the unknown but determined to get someone to care about your books and brochures, more captivating than anyone or anything I've seen in ages . . . you just made sense to me."

Miranda held the box in her palm. She didn't reopen it. But she stared at it. Whatever she was thinking, it wasn't negative enough to convince her to hand the box back.

"Did you have this just lying around the house?"

"I bought it for you."

"When? We just met."

"Right before our date."

She considered his answer but did not betray any emotion toward it, positive or negative.

"We need to get to know each other more," she said. "There's no way I can accept this until—"

"You can borrow it for now. Decide later."

Miranda deflated. Maybe the tension got the better of her, but she had to laugh at that one.

"You're something else."

"As are you."

She spent the next minute lifting the box, lowering it, lifting it, lowering, unsure what she wanted to do with it. Maybe she wanted to tuck it away. Maybe she wanted to see it once more.

As long as she wasn't about to throw it away, Douglas was fine to—

Miranda opened the box and stared at the ring.

Then she looked at him as he stared back at her. Up ahead, the clock's minute hand was three minutes from reaching the top.

Miranda shrugged.

"Oh, what the hell. Nothing will burn as hot as the first time."

She carefully took the ring out of the box and squeezed it onto her finger. Douglas didn't know her ring size, so he had to guess. It looked like a tight fit. But she managed to slide it past her knuckle. As the clock reached two minutes to midnight, she raised her hand in front of her face, then moved it over for Douglas to see, blocking his view of the clock. The diamond was small, but it sparkled.

"What do you think?" she asked.

"Perfect," he said. "How about you?"

"Crazy. But it's lovely." She lowered her hand, bringing the ring a little closer to herself as she stared at it. Then she brought it much closer and stared hard at the jewel. "Hey, is this cubic zirconium?"

Douglas felt his heart drop.

"Is it what?"

She poked at the diamond. It did nothing to scratch her skin.

"It's soft. How much did you pay for it?"

"I—"

"This is cubic zirconium." She laughed. "I'm sure of it. It's not even real."

"But I thought—"

"You went to Ritzy and Respectable, didn't you?"

Douglas frowned.

"How did you—"

"I sold them a brochure package a month ago. They're the only jewelry shop open late on New Year's Eve."

Douglas said nothing.

"All their jewelry is fake. Impressive, but still fake. Costume jewelry."

Douglas said nothing.

"How much did you pay for it? They're so overpriced."

Douglas said nothing.

Miranda laughed at him. Then she squeezed his arm.

"Okay, you might be an idiot," she said, "but we'll give this a shot. Why not? I'd be curious to see if you can prove yourself, be what you say you are."

Douglas snapped back to reality.

"I can prove myself."

"Great. Because if you don't, I could always kill you. Humanely, of course. I'll be a nurse, after all, with plenty of access to medications that disagree with you. Or pillows." She closed the box and stuffed it in her handbag. "Also, just so you know, I have a three-year-old son at home. You get me, you get both of us. Non-negotiable."

Douglas's heart felt another hammer against it. *Her what?*

"I must admit, I've been wondering what to do for him when his father walked out on us for that slut." She turned and smiled at Douglas. "Now I know."

The crowd around them started counting down. Whatever Miranda said next, Douglas couldn't hear. But she finally seemed content.

And when the crowd screamed "Happy New Year," she wrapped her arms around his neck and kissed him full on the lips.

Douglas was still thinking about what she'd just said to him, not so much about the possible murder if things didn't work out because that was probably just bluster, but about the other thing. It took him a few seconds to respond.

But then reality struck. Miranda was kissing him. Maybe not passionately. Her lips were stale against his, as if she were just performing on stage, no big deal. But it was still a kiss. At midnight on New Year's Eve. He had to wrap his arms around her and kiss her back, fulfill his part of the show. He'd have to process the stunner she'd just hit him with later.

He would have to process it. Later.

Was "now" considered the "later" to a second ago?

Miranda pulled away and smiled at him. It took him a couple of seconds to register what was happening. But his brain responded. He smiled back.

He knew little about being a partner, but he knew absolutely nothing about being a father. Nothing at all. Did he just volunteer to become one out of the blue? Like an idiot? Despite the cold, he felt sweat breaking the surface of his skin, especially around his neck.

What the hell had he just gotten himself into? What did he know about three-year-olds other than that they threw temper tantrums all the time?

When Douglas first met Miranda, Sally the office receptionist had warned him that Miranda would break his heart. Douglas thought she was overexaggerating the circumstances, but she'd cited past examples of women he'd just met that had captured him in such profound ways that he wanted to marry them on the spot. Even though he protested her error in thinking, he could see now that Sally wasn't wrong.

She'd told him to be careful, but he hadn't been. She thought he would rush Miranda into an uncomfortable situation, causing her to reject him, and that his impulse would leave him empty and alone yet again.

But neither of them had considered the price of success. That was the hidden monster that Douglas didn't realize was hiding behind the door.

Sally was wrong about the rejection, but she was right about the effect of Douglas's impulsiveness. If rejection and loneliness wouldn't drown him this time, then parenting someone else's child when he'd never even bought wall outlet cover would take the job instead.

"I'm glad I walked into your office last week," Miranda said, squeezing her hollow words into his screaming thoughts. "I suppose I'm ready to believe you."

"Great," he said.

Great, he thought.

When the crowds thinned out and they could move again, Douglas walked with Miranda through the courtyard and down the walkways toward her car. Not much was said along the way. Miranda stole glances at her new ring, but she looked more relaxed with every step she took. By the time they'd reached the street, she was taking steps in full stride with her chin held high.

But Douglas's gait became more tense. He felt his spine bending forward the closer he got to her car. He hoped Miranda couldn't sense the sudden shock he felt over what felt like a surprise attack. The last thing he wanted was to confirm her fears.

Mercifully, she pointed at a vehicle parked along the curb about thirty feet ahead.

"That's me," she said. "So, I guess we should think about our plans for the next date."

"Yeah."

"Call me in a few days?"

"Sure."

She reached for his hand and stroked it.

"I admit I was uneasy tonight. Well, for a lot of reasons, as I'm sure you can figure out. But I'm glad I came out."

Douglas smiled at her. He couldn't tell if his smile was enthusiastic or just visible.

"I'm also terrified if I'm being honest. I've never been this impulsive. Well, not quite in this way. Actually, the first time was a bit sudden, now that I think about it. But . . . yeah."

"Yeah."

"This is different, though. This isn't me being stupid and rebellious going after the hot bad boy like before. Maybe you're onto something about that 'just knowing.' Maybe I kinda just know, too."

"Maybe."

Hot bad boy?

She leaned in and kissed him on the cheek. When she pulled away, her eyes were bright. Her face was the most relaxed he'd seen since they'd met, and it was enough to melt his heart again. He still knew, even with the midnight surprise and potentially unfair comparison to a past lover.

He was pretty sure he still just knew.

"Maybe the couple at the airport in *Die Hard* got their happily ever after?" She reached out and squeezed his hand.

Despite the New Year's kiss and the shotgun pre-engagement, they were still on the first date, so this would be their tame goodnight. Douglas would have to kiss her more romantically next time, once they got past the initial sugar high and decided that they'd made the right decision choosing each other for the long haul.

And despite the tremors he felt through his skin and the realization of the oversized bite he'd just taken with his pseudo-proposal, he knew with certainty that there would be a next time. And a next time. And a next time.

So many next times.

He just didn't know how relaxed he would feel each time. At some point, he'd have to meet this kid. And he knew nothing of three-year-olds or how much he might accidentally scare them or break them.

Once Miranda got in her car and left, Douglas returned to his own.

Before he turned on the engine, he considered his situation. While his brain emptied into the silence, he caught a glimpse of his glove compartment. On a whim, he opened it.

Inside was the gift Miranda had given him at their departure on Christmas Eve. It was a small case with a vape pen inside.

Douglas had spent parts of the week contemplating whether to try it. But now that she'd accepted his major gift, he thought it was only fair that he'd accept her minor one.

So, he turned on his dome light, studied the shape and composition of the pen, loaded the flavor cartridge it came with, and took his first puff of electronic liquid smoke.

And just like that, as the chemicals from the pen entered his bloodstream and relaxed him, his fear of the future evaporated with the minty cloud that entered his cabin and dissipated.

No more stress. Nothing to worry about ever again. He decided he'd made the right decision tonight. He took another puff and savored the gift Miranda had given him.

~~~~~

~~~~~

And Now a Quick Message from the Author

The Story Continues in *The McCray Parables: Snow in Miami*, coming for the holiday season 2025. While you're waiting, subscribe to my newsletter to read the bonus short story "The Elf and the Shoe" and learn how Douglas McCray handles his landlady's rent demands on January 2nd after he's blown all his money on New Year's Eve. It will be available for download Christmas Eve 2024.

Note: You'll also get exclusive access to other bonus stories, including *Read My Shorts: Volume One* and future stories not yet written but will be soon.

https://swiy.co/jb-signup-mccray-fountain

Acknowledgments

Writing a book is hard. Sure, writing words is physically easy, but making those words say something important and truthful is hard, and when your personal experiences are limited, you must call in your outside resources to fill in the knowledge gaps to ensure the story remains authentic and accurate.

Therefore, I would like to thank Google and various chatbots like OpenAI's ChatGPT 4o model and Anthropic's Claude 3 Sonnet for help researching places, objects, materials, etc. I have no common knowledge of, ensuring I demonstrate some level of accuracy and understanding of my topics.

But because these are machines that demonstrate fake sincerity and have no real feeling or care that they've been used or acknowledged, and because they often hallucinate, presenting something false as true, I would like to also thank my human helpers who have feelings and don't hallucinate, who have given me feedback on the story or who will inevitably give me feedback after it goes to print (causing me to have to create a second edition).

To my human readers, thanks go to Ross Baylor for once again reading from start to finish and telling me the ending made the whole thing worth it. I'm not sure what that says about the rest of the story, but because the ending makes or breaks a book, I'm assuming the rest of the book is fine. Thanks for being honest about it.

I would also like to thank Michelle Gomez and Erin Berish for taking the time to screen the early version of this book. The problem with reading early versions is that they are never as good as the final product, so they must endure the book's worst form (that I allow others to read—obviously, I'm the one stuck reading the book's true worst form). So, thanks to them for their endurance and feedback.

I'd also like to thank readers of the original "The Fountain of Truth" short story (2005) and the subsequent *The Fountain of Truth* three-story e-book collection (2015) for their input on the original fables back when they were unaffiliated with Douglas McCray and his wacky cast of cohorts and just a series of fun, unrelated stories that taught readers a little something about Christmas, even if that little something was basically absurd. I know I'm taking a chance with sandwiching those old stories in with this new holiday series, but I think it works well. I wouldn't have done it otherwise.

And, finally, I'd like to thank you for reading the new version of *The Fountain of Truth*, and I hope you'll come back for its sequel, *Snow in Miami*, in 2025. Like *The Fountain of Truth*, *Snow in Miami* is a story I've lived with for years before finally making it public, so I will be happy to finally release it nine years after writing its first words. Please be sure to come back and read Douglas McCray's original first outing once *Snow in Miami* is released (or read it now if you are reading this in late 2025 or later). Subscribe to my newsletter if you want to ensure you don't miss it.

Note: If you've found errors with this book and would like to tell me about them, please visit my website at jeremybursey. com and send me a message through the contact form letting me know what you've found. Thanks.

Other Books

Want to discover what else I've written? Then visit my website and explore my library of titles to see what other books catch your eyes. You'll find them divided by genre and size, and you may even discover some freebies and discontinued books. It's the best way to discover my entire body of works, for better and for worse.

https://swiy.co/jb-books-mccray-fountain

The Golden Paperweight

He gave them an apple. They gave him a job.
All parties may soon come to regret it.

Lewis Urlong is a treasure hunter by trade. Relying on his years of skill, he can locate and liberate most relics in quick time. Once his handler arranges a buyer, Lewis gets into action, scouring whatever jungle, desert, or urban wasteland he must, to recover the client's most desired object. All that's left, then, is to deliver the prize, collect the payment, and move on to the next mission.

His latest assignment in the jungles of Guatemala breaks that routine. His job is to recover the Fruit of Huracan, or "the golden apple" as outsiders call it, a forbidden treasure from the ancient Maya Empire that hunters avoid, but the buyer goes MIA before Lewis can return it.

Now desperate to find a new buyer, Lewis offers the golden apple to the CEO of a fledgling investment company in Dallas who believes the apple will bring him luck. To ensure trouble doesn't come calling after the new owner, Lewis takes a job at the company to watch his back. "Trouble," of course, is Rory "The Jack" Sampson, the man responsible for the buyer's MIA status, a man on a mad mission to take the apple at any cost, a man neither Lewis nor the apple's new owner has yet met. And trouble is coming.

The Golden Paperweight is the upcoming comedic thriller from Jeremy Bursey that asks the question: What if Indiana Jones joined *The Office*?

About the Author

Jeremy Bursey is the author of many short stories, essays, and poems, along with a modest number of novels and screenplays, each covering topics and genres that differ from what he had written previously. He hopes to bring many of these into the e-book generation over the course of the next few years. He holds a bachelor's degree in English from the University of Central Florida and currently works at a local college as a writing tutor. He appreciates feedback for anything he offers to the public.

Visit him at jeremybursey.com
Or scan the QR Code to visit his smartpage biolink: